TOM SLADE
ON MYSTERY TRAIL

HERVEY LOOKED DOWN WHERE TOM POINTED AND SAW
LITTLE ANTHONY.

Tom Slade on Mystery Trail. *Frontispiece (Page 189)*

TOM SLADE
ON MYSTERY TRAIL

BY
PERCY KEESE FITZHUGH

Author of
TOM SLADE, BOY SCOUT, TOM SLADE AT TEMPLE
CAMP, ROY BLAKELEY, ETC.

ILLUSTRATED BY
R. EMMETT OWEN

Published with the approval of
THE BOY SCOUTS OF AMERICA

GROSSET & DUNLAP
PUBLISHERS : : NEW YORK

Made in the United States of America

CONTENTS

CHAPTER		PAGE
I	THE THREE SCOUTS	1
II	ANOTHER SCOUT	4
III	THE "ALL BUT" SCOUT	10
IV	HERVEY LEARNS SOMETHING . .	15
V	WHAT'S IN A NAME?	26
VI	THE EAGLE AND THE SCOUT . . .	31
VII	THE STREAK OF RED	35
VIII	EAGLE AND SCOUT	38
IX	TO INTRODUCE ORESTES	44
X	OFF WITH THE OLD LOVE, ON WITH THE NEW	48
XI	OFF ON A NEW TACK	57
XII	AS LUCK WOULD HAVE IT . . .	62
XIII	THE STRANGE TRACKS	67
XIV	HERVEY'S TRIUMPH	72
XV	SKINNY'S TRIUMPH	77
XVI	IN DUTCH	83
XVII	HERVEY GOES HIS WAY	91
XVIII	THE DAY BEFORE	96
XIX	THE GALA DAY	102

CONTENTS

CHAPTER		PAGE
XX	Uncle Jeb	109
XXI	The Full Salute	113
XXII	Tom Runs the Show	119
XXIII	Pee-Wee Settles It	123
XXIV	The Red Streak	132
XXV	The Path of Glory	141
XXVI	Mysterious Marks	147
XXVII	The Greater Mystery	152
XXVIII	Watchful Waiting	156
XXIX	The Wandering Minstrel . .	161
XXX	Hervey Makes a Promise . . .	169
XXXI	Sherlock Nobody Holmes . . .	175
XXXII	The Beginning of the Journey .	179
XXXIII	The Climb	185
XXXIV	The Rescue	188
Chapter the Last. Y-Extra! Y-Extra! . .		194

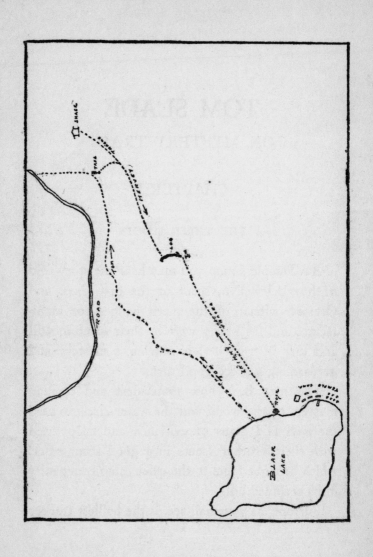

TOM SLADE

ON MYSTERY TRAIL

CHAPTER I

THE THREE SCOUTS

At Temple Camp you may hear the story told of how Llewellyn, scout of the first class, and Orestes, winner of the merit badges for architecture and for music, were by their scouting skill and lore instrumental in solving a mystery and performing a great good turn.

You may hear how these deft and cunning masters of the wood and the water circumvented the well laid plans of evil men and coöperated with their brother scouts in a good scout stunt, which brought fame to the quiet camp community in its secluded hills.

For one, as you shall see, is the bulliest tracker

that ever picked his way down out of a tangled wilderness and through field and over hill straight to his goal.

And the other is a famous gatherer of clews, losing sight of no significant trifle, as the scout saying is, and a star scout into the bargain, if we are to believe Pee-wee Harris. I am not so sure that the ten merit badges of bugling, craftsmanship, architecture, aviation, carpentry, camping, forestry, music, pioneering and signaling should be awarded this sprightly scout (for Pee-wee is as liberal with awards as he is with gumdrops). But there can be no question as to the propriety of the music and architecture awards, and I think that the aviation award would be quite appropriate also.

Yet if you should ask old Uncle Jeb Rushmore, beloved manager of the big scout camp, about these two scout heroes, a shrewd twinkle would appear in his eye and he would refer you to the boys, who would probably only laugh at you, for they are a bantering set at Temple Camp and would jolly the life out of Daniel Boone himself if that redoubtable woodsman were there.

Listen then while I tell you of how Tom Slade,

friend and brother of these two scouts, as he is of all scouts, assisted them, and of how they assisted him; and of how, out of these reciprocal good turns, there came true peace and happiness, which is the aim and end of all scouting.

CHAPTER II

ANOTHER SCOUT

IT was characteristic of Tom Slade that he liked to go off alone occasionally for a ramble in the woods. It was not that he liked the scouts less, but rather that he liked the woods more. It was his wont to stroll off when his camp duties for the day were over and poke around in the adjacent woods.

The scouts knew and respected his peculiarities and preferences, particularly those who were regular summer visitors at the big camp, and few ever followed him into his chosen haunts. Occasionally some new scout, tempted by the pervading reputation and unique negligee of Uncle Jeb's young assistant, ventured to follow him and avail himself of the tips and woods lore with which the more experienced scout's conversation abounded when he was in talking mood. But Tom was a sort of creature apart and the boys of camp, good scouts that they were, did not intrude upon his lonely rambles.

The season was well nigh over at Temple Camp when this thing happened. Not over exactly, but the period of arrivals had passed and the period of departures would begin in a day or two—as soon as the events with which the season culminated were over.

These were the water events, the tenderfoot carnival (not to be missed on any account) and the big affair at the main pavilion when awards were to be made. This last, in particular, would be a gala demonstration, for Mr. John Temple himself, founder of the big scout camp, had promised to be on hand to dedicate the new tract of camp property and personally to distribute the awards.

These events would break the backbone of the camping season, high schools and grammar schools would presently beckon their reluctant conscripts back to town and city, until, in the pungent chill of autumn, old Uncle Jeb, alone among the boarded-up cabins, would smoke his pipe in soli\ tude and get ready for the long winter.

It was late on Thursday afternoon. The last stroke of the last hammer, where scouts had been erecting a rustic platform outside the pavilion, had echoed from the neighboring hills. The usually still water of the lake was rippled by the refreshing breeze which heralded a cooler evening, and the first rays of dying sunlight painted the ripples golden, and bathed the cone-like tops of the fir trees across the lake with a crimson glow.

Out of the chimney of the cooking shack arose the smoke of early promise, from which the scouts deduced various conclusions as to the probable character of the meal which would appear in all its luscious glory a couple of hours later.

A group of scouts, weary of diving, were strung along the springboard which overhung the shore. A couple of boys played mumbly-peg under the bulletin board tree. Several were playing ball with an apple, until one of them began eating it, which put an end to the game. Half a dozen of the older boys, who had been at work erecting the platform, sauntered toward the scrub shack, leaving one or two to festoon the bunting over the stand where the colors shone as if they had been varnished by that master decorator, the sun, as a last finishing touch to his sweltering day's work. The emblem patrol sauntered over to the flag pole and sprawled beneath it to rest and await the moment of sunset. Several canoes moved aimlessly upon the glinting water, their occupants idling with the paddles. It was the time of waiting, the empty hour or two between the day's end and supper-time.

Upon a rock near the lake sat a little fellow, quite alone. He was very small and very thin, and his belt was drawn ridiculously tight, so that it gave his khaki jacket the effect of being shirred like the top of a cloth bag. If he had been standing, he might have suggested, not a little, the shape of an old-fashioned hour glass. A brass compass dangled around his neck on a piece of twine as if, being so small, he was in danger of getting lost any minute. His hair was black and very streaky, and his eyes had a strange brightness in them.

No one paid any attention to this little gnome of a boy, and he was a pathetic sight sitting there

with his intense gaze, having just a touch of wild-
ness in it, fixed upon the lake. Doubtless if his
scout regalia had fitted him properly he would
not have seemed so pathetic, for it is not uncom-
mon for a scout to want to be alone in the great
companionable wilderness.

Suddenly, this little fellow's gaze was with-
drawn from the lake and fell upon something
which seemed to interest him right at his feet. He
slid down from the rock and examined it closely.
His poor little thin figure and skinny legs were
very noticeable then. But he picked up nothing,
only kneeled there, apparently in a state of great
excitement and elation.

Presently, he started away, looked back, as if
he was afraid his discovery would take advantage
of his absence to steal away. Again he started,
hurrying around the edge of the cooking shack
and to the little avenue of patrol cabins beyond.
As he hurried along, the big brass compass flopped
about and sometimes banged against his belt
buckle, making quite a noise. Several boys
laughed as he passed them, trotting along as if
possessed by a vision. But no one stopped him
or spoke to him.

In the patrol cabin where he belonged, he rooted in great haste and excitement among the contents of a cheap pasteboard suit case and presently pulled out a torn and battered old copy of the scout handbook. He sat down on the edge of his cot and, hurriedly looking through the index, opened the book at page thirty. He was breathing so hard that he almost gulped, and his thin little hands trembled visibly. . . .

CHAPTER III

THE "ALL BUT" SCOUT

In that same hour, perhaps a little earlier or later, I cannot say, Tom Slade, having finished his duties for the day, strolled along the lake shore away from camp and struck into the woods which extended northward as far as the Dansville road.

He had no notion of where he was going; he was going nowhere in particular. For aught I know he was going to ponder on the responsibility which had been thrust upon him by the scout powers that be, of judging stalking photographs preliminary to awarding the Audubon prize offered by the historical society in his home town. Perhaps he was under the influence of a little pensive regret that the season was coming to an end and wished to have this lonely parting with his beloved hills and trees. It is of no consequence. About all he actually did was to kick a stick along before him and pause now and again to examine the caked green moss on trees.

When he had reached a little eminence whence the view behind him was unobstructed, he turned and looked down upon the camp. Perhaps in that brief glimpse the whole panorama of his adventurous life spread before him in his mind's eye, and he saw the vicious little hoodlum that he had once been transformed into a scout, pass through the several ranks of scouting, grow up, go to war, and come back to be assistant at the camp where he had spent so many happy hours when he was a young boy.

And now there was not one thing down there, nor shack nor cabin nor shooting range nor boat nor canoe, nor hero's elm (as they called it), nor Gold Cross Rock, which had the same romantic interest as had this young fellow to the scouts who came in droves and watched him and listened to the talk about him and dreamed of being just such a real scout as he. He moved about unconsciously among them, simple, childlike, stolid, but with a kind of assurance and serenity which he may have learned from the woods.

He was singularly oblivious to the superficial appurtenances of scouting. He had passed through that stage. The pomp and vanity of the tenderfoot he knew not. The bespangled dignity of the second-class and first-class scout, these things he had known and outgrown. His medals were home somewhere. And out of all this alluring rigmarole and romantic glory were left the deeper marks of scout training, burned into his soul as the mark is burned into the skin of a broncho. The woods, the trees, were his. That, after all, is the highest award in scouting. It is a medal that one does not lose, and it lasts forever.

As Tom Slade stood there looking down upon the camp, one might have seen in him the last and fullest accomplishment of scouting, stripped of all else. His face was the color of a mulatto. He wore no scout hat, he wore no hat at all. It would have been quite superfluous for him to have worn any of his thirty or forty merit badges of fond memory on his sleeves, for his sleeves were rolled up to his shoulders. He wore a pongee shirt, this being a sort of compromise between a shirt and nothing at all. He wore moccasins, but not Indian moccasins. He was still partial to khaki trousers, and these were worn with a strange contraption for a belt; it was a kind of braided fiber of his own manufacture, the material of which was said to have been taken from a string tree.

As he resumed his way through the woods he presently heard a cheery, but rather exhausted, voice behind him.

"Have a heart, Slady, and wait a minute, will you?" Tom's pursuer called. "I'm nearly dead climbing up through all this jungle after you. Old Mother Nature's got herself into a fine mess of a tangle through here, hey? Don't mind if I come along with you, do you? Look down there, hey? Pavilion looks nice. I've been wondering if I stand any chance of being called up on that platform on Saturday night. Looks swell with all the bunting over it, doesn't it?"

The speaker, who had been half talking and half shouting, now came stumbling and panting up over the edge of the wooded decline where the thick brush had played havoc with his scout suit but not with his temper.

"Some climb, hey?" he breathed, laughing, and affecting the stagger of utter exhaustion. "I bet you knew an easier way up. The bunch told me not to beard the lion in his den, but I'm not afraid of lions. Here I am and you can't get rid of me now. I'm up against it, Slady, and I want a few tips. They say you're the only real scout since Kit Carson. What I'm hunting for is a wild animal, but I haven't been able to find anything except a cricket, two beetles and a cow that belongs on the Hasbrook farm. Don't mind if I stroll along with you a little way, do you? My name is Willetts—Hervey Willetts. I'm with that troop from Massachusetts. I'm an Eagle Scout—*all but*."

"But's a pretty big word," Tom said.

"You said it," Hervey Willetts said, still wrestling with his breath; "it's the biggest word in the dictionary."

CHAPTER IV

HERVEY LEARNS SOMETHING

THEY strolled on through the woods together, the younger boy's gayety and enthusiasm showing in pleasing contrast to Tom's stolid manner.

He was a wholesome, vivacious boy, this Willetts, with a breeziness which seemed to captivate even his sober companion, and if Tom had felt any slight annoyance at being thus overhauled by a comparative stranger, the feeling quickly passed in the young scout's cheery company.

"They told me down in camp that if I need a guide, philosopher, and friend, I'd better run you down, or up——"

"If you'd gone a little to the left you'd have found it easier," Tom said, in his usual matter-of-fact manner.

"Oh, I suppose you know all the highways and byways and right ways and left ways and every which ways for miles and miles around," Hervey Willetts said. "I guess they were right when they said you'd be a good guide, philosopher, and friend, hey?"

"I don't know what a philosopher is," Tom said, with characteristic blunt honesty, "but I know all the trails around here, if that's what you're talking about."

"Oh, you mean about guides?" Hervey asked, just a trifle puzzled. "That's an expression, *guide, philosopher, and friend*. It comes from Shakespeare or one of those old ginks; it means a kind of a moral guide, I suppose."

"Oh," said Tom.

"But I need, I need, I need, I need a friend," Hervey said.

"You seem to have lots of friends down there," Tom said.

"A scout is observant, hey?" Willetts laughed.

"I mean you always seem to have a lot of fellows with you," Tom said, ignoring the compliment. "Everybody likes your troop, that's sure. And your troop seems to be stuck on *you*."

"Good night!" Hervey laughed. "They won't be stuck on me after Saturday. That'll be the end of my glorious career."

"What did you do?" Tom asked, after his customary fashion of construing talk literally.

"Oh, I didn't exactly commit a murder," the other laughed, "but I fell down, Sla—you don't mind my calling you Slady, do you?"

"That's what most everybody calls me," Tom said, "except the troop I was in. They call me Tomasso."

"Sounds like tomato, hey?" Hervey laughed. "No, my troubles are about merit badges. I've bungled the whole thing up. When a fellow goes after the Eagle award, he ought to have a manager, that's what I say. He ought to have a manager to plan things out for him. I tried to manage my own campaign and now I'm stuck— with a capital S."

"How many merits have you got?" Tom asked him.

"Twenty," Hervey said, "twenty and two-thirds. Just a fraction more and I'd have gone over the top."

"You mean a sub-division?" Tom asked.

"That's where the little *but* comes in," Hervey said. "B-u-t, but. It's a big word, all right, just as you said."

"Is it architecture or cooking or interpreting or one of those?" Tom asked.

Hervey glanced at Tom in frank surprise.

"Maybe it's leather work, or machinery, or taxidermy or marksmanship," Tom continued, with no thought further from his mind than that of showing off.

"Guess again," Hervey laughed.

"Then it must be either music or stalking," Tom said, dully.

His companion paused in his steps, contemplating Tom with unconcealed amazement. "Right-o," he said; "it's stalking. What are you? A mind reader?"

"Those are the only ones that have three tests," Tom said. "So if you have twenty merits and two-thirds of a merit, why, you must be trying for one of those. Maybe they've changed it since I looked at the handbook."

Hervey Willetts stood just where he had stopped, looking at Tom with admiration. In his astonishment he glanced at Tom's arm as if he expected to see upon it the tangible evidences of his companion's feats and accomplishments. But the only signs of scouting which he saw there were the brown skin and the firm muscles.

"They change that book every now and then," Tom said.

Still Hervey continued to look. "What's that belt made out of?" he asked.

"It's fiber from a string tree," Tom said; "they grow in Lorraine in France."

"Were you in France?"

"Two years," Tom said.

"How many merit badges have you got, anyway, Mr.—Slady?"

"Oh, I don't know," Tom said; "about thirty or thirty-five, I guess."

"You *guess?* I bet you've got the Gold Cross. Where is it?" Hervey made a quick inspection of Tom's pongee shirt, but all he saw there was the front with buttons gone and the brown chest showing.

"I couldn't pin it on there very well, could I?" Tom said, lured by his companion's eagerness into a little show of amusement.

"Where is it?" Hervey demanded.

"I'm letting a girl wear it," Tom said.

"Oh, what I know about *you!*" Hervey said, teasingly. "You can bet if I ever get the Gold Cross or the Eagle Badge (which I won't this trip) no girl will ever wear them."

"You can't be so sure about that," said Tom, out of his larger worldly experience, "sometimes they take them away from you."

"You're a funny fellow," Hervey said, while his gaze still expressed his generous impulse of hero-worship. "I guess I seem like just a sort of kid to you with my twenty merits—twenty and two-thirds. Maybe some girl is wearing your Distinguished Service Cross, for all I know. But we fellows are crazy to have the Eagle award in our troop. I suppose of course you're an Eagle Scout?"

"I guess that was about three or four years ago," Tom said.

"Once a scout, always a scout, hey?"

"That's it," Tom said.

They strolled along in silence for a few minutes, Hervey occasionally stealing a side glimpse at his elder, who ambled on, apparently unconscious of these admiring glances. Now and again Tom paused to examine a patch of moss or some little tell-tale mark upon the ground, as if he had no knowledge of his companion's presence. But Hervey appeared quite satisfied.

"I'll tell you how it is," he finally said, selecting what seemed an appropriate moment to speak; "I was elected as the one in our troop to go after the Eagle award. We want an Eagle Scout in our troop. We haven't even got one in the city where I live."

"Hear that?" Tom said. "That's a thrush."

"A thrush?"

"Yop; go on," Tom said.

"So they elected me to win the Eagle award. Some choice, hey? I had seven badges to begin with; maybe that's why they wished it onto me. I had camping, cooking, athletics, pioneering, angling, that's a cinch, that's easy, and, let's see —carpentry and bugling. That's the easiest one of the lot, just blow through the cornet and claim the badge. It's a shame to take it."

"You mean you've won thirteen more since you've been here?" Tom asked.

"That's it," said Hervey. "First I got my fists

on the eleven that have *got* to be included in the twenty-one, and then I made up a list of ten others and went to it. I chose easy ones, but some of them didn't turn out to be so easy. Music—oh, boy! And when I started to play the piano, they said I wasn't playing at all, but that I really meant it. Can you beat that?"

Tom could not help smiling.

"So you see I've been pretty busy since I've been here, too busy to talk to interviewers, hey? I've piled up thirteen since I've been here; that's a little over six weeks. That isn't so bad, is it?"

"It's good," Tom said, by no means carried away by enthusiasm.

"I thought you'd say so. So now I've got twenty and I know them all by heart. Want to hear me stand up in front of the class and say them?"

"All right," Tom said.

"No sooner said than stung," Hervey flung back at him. "Well, I've got first aid, physical development, life saving, personal health, public health, cooking, camping, bird study——"

"That's a good one," Tom said.

"You said it; and I've got pioneering, path-finding, athletics, and then come the ten that I selected myself; angling, bugling, carpentry, conservation or whatever you call it, and cycling and firemanship and music hath charms, not, and seamanship and signaling. And two-thirds of the stalking badge. I bet you'll say that's a good one."

"There's one good one that you left out," Tom said. "I thought you'd think of it on account of that last one."

"You mean stalking?"

"I mean another that has something to do with that?"

"Now you've got me guessing," Hervey said.

"Well, how do you want me to help you?" Tom asked, thus stifling his companion's inquisitiveness.

"Well," said Hervey, ready, even eager to adapt himself to Tom's mood, "all I've got to do is to track an animal for a half a mile or so——"

"A quarter of a mile," Tom said.

"And then I'm an Eagle Scout," Hervey concluded. "But if I want to be in on the hand-outs Saturday night, I've got to do it between now and Saturday, and that's what has me worried. I want to go home from here an Eagle Scout. Gee, I don't want all my work to go for nothing."

"You want what you want when you want it, don't you?" Tom said, smiling a little.

"It's on account of my troop, too," Hervey said. "It isn't just myself that I'm thinking about. Jiminies, maybe I didn't choose the best ones, you know more about the handbook than I do, that's sure, and I suppose that one badge was just as easy as another to *you*. Maybe you think I just chose easy ones, hey?"

"Well, what's on your mind?" Tom said.

"Do you know where there are any wild animal tracks?" Hervey blurted out with amusing simplicity. "I don't mean just exactly where, but do you know a good place to hunt for any? A couple of fellows told me you would know, because you know everything of that sort. So I thought maybe you could give me a tip where to look. I found a horseshoe last night so maybe I'll be lucky. All I want is to get started on a trail."

"Sometimes there are different trails and they take you to the same place," Tom said.

No doubt this was one of the sort of remarks

that Tom was famous for making which had either no particular meaning or a meaning poorly expressed.

Hervey stared at him for a few seconds, then said, "I don't care whether it's easy or hard, if that's what you mean.   Is it true that there are wild cats up in these mountains?"

"Some," Tom said.

"Well, if you were in my place, where would you go to look for a trail? I mean a real trail, not a cow or a horse or Chocolate Drop's kitten.* If I can just dig up the trail of a wild animal somewhere, right away quick, the Eagle award is mine—ours. See? Can you give me a tip?"

Tom's answer was characteristic of him and it was not altogether satisfactory.

"I'm not so stuck on eagles," he said.

---

* Chocolate Drop was the negro cook at Temple Camp.

CHAPTER V

WHAT'S IN A NAME?

"You're not?" Hervey asked in puzzled dismay. "You can bet that every time I look at that little old gold eagle on top of the flag pole I say, 'Me for you, kiddo.'"

"I like Star Scout better," Tom said, unmoved by his companion's consternation.

"Why, that means only ten merit badges," Hervey said.

"It's fun studying the stars," Tom added.

"Oh, sure," Hervey agreed. "But star and eagle, they're just names. What's in a name, hey? Is that the badge you meant that I forgot about? The astronomy badge?"

"No, it isn't," Tom said. "You're too excitable to study the stars. It's got to be something livelier."

"You've got me down pat, that's sure," Hervey laughed.

Tom smiled, too. "Well, you want the Eagle badge, do you?" he said.

"You seem to think it doesn't amount to much," Hervey complained.

"I think it amounts to a whole lot," Tom said.

"When I get my mind on a thing——" Hervey announced.

"That's the trouble with you," Tom said.

"There you go," Hervey shot back at him; "you've been through the game and walked away with every honor in the book, and you know the book by heart and you can track with your eyes shut and you've been to France and all that and you think I'm just a kid, but it means something to be an Eagle Scout, I can tell you."

Doubtless Tom Slade, scout, was gratified to receive this valuable information. "And there's just the one way to get there, is that it?" he answered quietly, but smiling a little. "I always heard that a scout was resourceful and had two strings to his bow."

"You just give me a tip and I'll do the rest," said Hervey.

"It must be about tracking, hey?"

"That's it; test three for the stalking badge. *Track an animal a quarter of a mile.*"

"Well, let me think a minute, then," Tom said.

"Up on that mountain, maybe, hey?" Hervey urged.

"Maybe," Tom said.

So they ambled along, the elder quite calm and thoroughly master of himself, the younger, all impulse, eagerness and enthusiasm. His generous admiration of Tom, amounting almost to a spirit of worship, was plainly to be seen. It would have been hard to say how Tom felt or what he thought. At all events he had not been jostled out of his stolid calm.

"Did you ever hear any one say that there is more than one way to kill a cat?" he finally inquired, pausing to notice some bird or squirrel among the trees.

"I don't want to kill a cat," Hervey said. "I want to find some tracks, I——"

"You want to be an Eagle Scout," Tom concluded; "and you've got your mind set on it. That it?"

"That's it; but it's for the sake of my troop, too."

Still again, they strolled on in silence. A little twig cracked under Tom's foot, the crackle sounding clear in the solemn stillness. Some feathered creature chirped complainingly at the rude intrusion of its domain by these strangers. And, almost under their very feet, a tiny snake wriggled across the trail and was gone. The shadows were gathering now, and the fragrance of evening was beginning to permeate the dim woods. And all the respectable home-loving birds were seeking their nests.

And so these two strolled on, and for a few minutes neither spoke.

"Well then, suppose I give you a tip," Tom said. "Will you promise that you'll make good? You claim to be a scout. You say that when you get your mind set on a thing, nothing can stop you. That the idea?"

"That's it," Hervey answered.

"You wouldn't drop a trail after you once picked it up, would you? Some animals take you pretty far."

"You bet nothing would stop *me* if I once got the tracks," Hervey said. "I wouldn't care if they took me across the Desert of Sahara or over the Rocky Mountains."

"Hang on like a bulldog, hey?" Tom said.

"That's me," said Hervey.

"All right, it's a go," Tom concluded. "I'll see if I can give you a pointer or two down near camp in the morning. Ever follow a woodchuck— or a coon? Only I don't want any badge-getter falling down on a trail, if I'm mixed up with it. That's one thing I can't stand—a quitter."

"I wouldn't anyway," Hervey said with great fervor; "but as long as I've got you and what you said to think about, you can bet your sweet life that not even a—a—a jungle would stop me—it wouldn't."

"That's the kind of a fellow they want for an Eagle Scout," Tom said; "do or die."

"That's me," said Hervey Willetts.

CHAPTER VI

THE EAGLE AND THE SCOUT

AND so these two strolled on. And presently they came to a point where the wood was more sparse, for they were approaching the rugged lower ledges of a mighty mountain, and the last rays of the dying sun fell upon the rocks and scantier vegetation of this clearer area, emphasizing the solemn darkness of the wooded ascent beyond.

Few, even of the scouts, had ever penetrated the enshrouding wilderness of that dizzy, forbidding height. There were strange tales, usually told to tenderfeet around the camp-fire, of mysterious hermits and ferocious bears and half-savage men who lurked high up in those all but inaccessible fastnesses, but no scout from Temple Camp had ever ascended beyond the lower reaches of that frowning old monarch.

At Temple Camp, when the cheery blaze was crackling in the witching hour of yarn telling, the seasoned habitués of the camp would direct the eye of the newcomer to a little glint of light high up upon the mountain, and edify him with dark tales of a lonesome draft dodger who had challenged that tangled profusion of tree and brush to escape going to war and had never been able to find his way down again—a quite just punishment for his cowardice. But time and again this freakish glint of light had been proven to be the reflection of that very camp-fire upon a huge rock lodged up there and held by interlacing roots.

Tom and Hervey stood upon a ledge of rock just outside the area of a great elm tree, and as they looked down and afar off, Black Lake seemed a mere puddle with toy cabins near it.

"I bet there are wild animals up there," Hervey said.

"Here's one of them now," commented Tom, pointing upward.

High above them in the dusk and with a background of golden-edged clouds, which gave the sun's last parting message to the earth, a great bird hovered motionless. It seemed to hang in air as if by a thread. Then it descended with a wide, circling swoop. In less than ten seconds, as it seemed to Hervey, its body and great wings, and even its curved, cruel beak, were plainly visible circling a few yards above the tree. It seemed like a journey from the heavens to the earth, all in an instant.

"Watch him, watch him," Hervey whispered.

But Tom was not watching him at all. He knew what that savage descent meant and he was looking for its cause. Stealthily, with no more sound than that of a gliding canoe, he stole to the trunk of the tree and looked about with quick, short, scrutinizing glances, away up among its branches.

Then he placed his finger to his lips, warning Hervey to silence, and beckoned him into the darker shadow under the great tree.

"Did you see anything beside the bird?" he whispered.

"No," said Hervey. "Why? What is it?"

"Shh," Tom said; "look up—shh——"

It was the most fateful moment of all Hervey Willetts' scout career, and he did not know it.

CHAPTER VII

THE STREAK OF RED

"Look up there," Tom said; "out near the end of the third branch. See? The little codger beat him to it."

Looking up, Hervey saw amid the thicker foliage, far removed from the stately trunk, something hanging from a leaf-covered branch. Even as he looked at it, it seemed to be swaying as if from a recent jolt. At first glimpse he thought it was a bat hanging there.

"See it?" Tom said, pointing up. "You can see it by the little streak of red. I think the little codger's head is poking out. Some scare she had."

Then all in an instant Hervey knew. It seemed incredible that the great bird, hovering at that dizzy height, could have seen the little songster

35

of the woods which even he and Tom had failed to see. And the thought of that smaller bird reaching its home just in time, and poking its head out of the opening to see if all was well, went to Hervey's heart and stirred a sudden anger within him.

"I didn't know they could see all that distance," he said.

"Well, that's one thing you've learned that you didn't know before," Tom said in his matter-of-fact way.

Scarcely had he spoken the words when the foliage above shook and there was a loud rustling and crackling of branches, while many leaves and twigs fell to the ground.

The monarch of the mountain crags, having circled the elm, had found a way in where the foliage was least dense, and had thus with irresistible power carried the outer defenses of that little hanging citadel.

And still the little streak of red showed up there in the dimness of those invaded branches, and one might have fancied it to be the colors of the besieged victim, flaunting still in a kind of hopeless defiance. Down out of the green twilight above floated a feather, then another—trifling losses of the conqueror in his triumphal entry.

"You're not going to get away with that," said Hervey in a voice tense with wrath and grim determination; "you're—you're—not——"

What happened then happened so quickly as almost to rival the descent of the destroyer in lightning movement. Before Tom Slade realized what had happened, there was Hervey's khaki jacket on the ground, his discarded hat was blowing away, and his navy blue scout scarf was plastered by the freshening breeze flat against the trunk of the tree.

Hervey Willetts, who had dreamed and striven all through the vacation season of "capturing the Eagle," as they say, was on his quest in dead earnest.

CHAPTER VIII

EAGLE AND SCOUT

Up, up, he went, now reaching like a monkey, now wriggling like a snake. Now he loosed one hand to sweep back the hair which fell over his forehead. Again, unable to release his hold, he threw his head back to shake away the annoying locks. Tom Slade, stolid though he was, watched him, thrilled with amazement and admiration.

The great bird was embarrassed in the confines of the foliage by its big wings. But the freedom and strength of its cruel beak and talons were unimpaired and every second brought it nearer to the hanging nest.

But every second brought also the scout nearer to the hanging nest. Up, up he went, now straddling some bending limb, now swinging himself with lightning agility to one above. Once, crawling on a horizontal branch, he slid over and hung beneath it, like an opossum.

Twisting and wriggling his way out of this predicament, he scrambled on, handing himself from branch to branch, and once losing his foothold and hanging by one hand.

Tom Slade watched spellbound, as the agile form ascended, using every physical device and disregarding every danger. More than once Tom almost shuddered at the chances which his young companion took upon some perilously slender limb. Once, the impulse seized him to call a warning, but he refrained from a kind of inspired confidence in that young dare-devil who by now seemed a mere speck of brown moving in and out of the darkened green above him. Once he was on the point of shouting advice to Hervey about what to do in the unlikely event of his reaching the nest before the eagle, or in the more serious contingency of an encounter with that armed warrior.

For, thrilled as he was at the young scout's agility and fine abandon, he was yet doubtful of Hervey's power of deliberation and presence of mind. But no one could advise a creature capable of being carried away in a very frenzy of nervous enthusiasm, and Tom, sober and sensible, knew this. Hervey Willetts would do this thing or crash his brains out, one or the other, and no one could help or hinder him.

Amid the crackling sound of breaking limbs and a shower of leaves and smaller twigs, the mighty bird of prey, extricating himself from every obstacle, tore his way into the leafy recess where his little victim waited, trembling. Every branch seemed agitated by his ruthless, irresistible advance, and the hanging nest swayed upon its slender branch, as the cruel talons of the intruder fixed themselves in the yielding bark. The weight of the monster bird upon the very branch which his little victim had chosen for a home caused it to bend almost to the breaking point, and the hanging nest, agitated by the shock, swung low near the end of the curving bough.

That was bad strategy on the part of the invader. As the end of the bough descended under his weight, there was the appalling sound of a splitting branch, which made Tom Slade's blood run cold, and he held his breath in frightful

HERVEY SAVES THE LITTLE BIRD FROM THE EAGLE.

Tom Slade on Mystery Trail.   *Page* 42

suspense, expecting to see the form of his young friend come crashing to earth.

But the boy who had ventured out so far upon that straining branch had swung free of it just in time, and was swinging from the branch above. The great bird had played into the hands of his dexterous enemy when he had placed his weight upon the branch above, from which the nest hung.

Hervey could not have trusted his own weight upon that upper branch, and he knew it. But even had he dared to do this he could not have passed the enraged bird who stood guard within a yard or two of his little victim. When the weight of the bird's great body bent the branch down, Hervey, close in toward the trunk just below, saw his chance. He did not see the danger.

Scrambling out upon that slender branch, he moved cautiously but with beating heart, out to a point where the bending branch above was within his reach. If the eagle had left the branch above, that branch would have swung out of Hervey's reach and he would have gone crashing to the ground when his own branch broke. He knew that branch must break under him. He knew, he *must* have known, that the chances were at least even that the eagle would desert the branch above in either assault or flight.

Hervey's chance was the chance of a moment, and it lay just in this: in getting far enough out on the branch before it broke to catch the branch above before it sprang up and away from him. Also he must trust to the slightly heavier branch above not breaking.

It would be impossible to say by what a narrow squeak he saved himself in this dare-devil maneuver. His one chance lay in lightning agility.

Yet, first and last, it was an act of fine and desperate recklessness—the recklessness of a soul possessed and set on one dominating purpose. This was Hervey Willetts all over. And because he had a brain and the eagle none or little, he thus used his very enemy to help him accomplish his purpose.

In that very moment when Tom Slade heard with a shudder the appalling sound of that splitting branch, something beside the brown nest was also dangling from the branch which the baffled eagle had suddenly deserted. Right close to the swaying nest the boy hung, his limbs encircling it, his two hands locked upon it, trusting to it, just trusting to it. It bent low in a great sweeping curve, the nest swayed and swung from the movement of the swing downward, a little olive-colored, speckled head peeking cautiously out as if to see what all the rumpus was about.

It must have seemed to those little frightened eyes that the familiar geography of the neighborhood was radically changed. But there was nothing near to strike terror to it now. There was nothing near but the green, enshrouding foliage, and the brown object hanging almost motionless close by.

This was Hervey Willetts of the patrol of the blue scarf, scout of the first class (if ever there was one) and winner of twenty-one merit badges. . . .

No, not twenty-one. Twenty and two-thirds.

CHAPTER IX

TO INTRODUCE ORESTES

HERVEY moved cautiously in along the limb to a point where he felt sure that it would hold his weight, and as he did so it moved slowly up into place. What the little householder thought of all this topsy-turvy business it might be amusing to know. For surely, if the world war changed the map of Europe, the little neighborhood of leaf and branch where this timid denizen of the woods lived and had its being, had been subject to jolts and changes quite as sweeping. Now and again it poked its downy speckled head out for a kind of disinterested squint at things, apparently unconcerned with mighty upheavals so long as its little home was undisturbed.

Hervey Willetts straddled the branch and calculated the thickness of it.

"You all right?" he heard Tom call from below.

"Yop," he called back; "did you see his nobs fly away? Back to the crags for him, hey? Wait down there a few minutes, I'm going to bring a friend."

Hervey had now a very nice little calculation to make. In the first place he must not frighten his new acquaintance by approaching too near again. Neither must he make any sudden and unnecessary noise or motions. He knew that a nest of that particular sort was more than a home, it was a comparatively safe refuge, and he knew that its occupant would not emerge and desert it without good cause. One of those precious twenty badges was evidence of that much knowledge.

His purpose was to cut the branch as near to the nest as he dared, both from the standpoint of the bird's peace of mind and his own safety. The further from the nest he cut, the thicker would be the branch, and the more cutting there would be to do. To cut too near to the nest might frighten his little neighbor on the branch, and endanger his own life.

Yet if he cut the branch where it was thick, how

could he handle it after it was detached? How would he get down with it through all that network of lower branches?

In his quandary he hit on a plan involving new peril for himself and doubtless some agitation to his little neighbor. He would not detach the nest from its branch, for how could he ever attach it to another branch in a way satisfactory to that finicky little householder? He knew enough about his business to know that no bird would continue to live in a nest which had been tampered with to that extent.

So he advanced cautiously out on the branch again till he could reach the nest. Then very gently he bound his handkerchief about the opening. Having done this, he cut into the branch with his scout knife within about six or eight inches of the nest. When he had cut the branch almost through it was a pretty ticklish matter, straddling the stubby end, for he had the tip of the branch with the nest still in his hand and was in danger of losing his balance.

Sitting there with his legs pressed up tight against the under side of the branch so as to hold his balance on his precarious seat, he held the end in one hand while he carefully pulled away the twigs from the end beyond the nest. Thus he had a piece of branch perhaps twenty inches long, with the nest hanging midway of it. This he held with the greatest care, lest in turning the branch the delicate fabric by which it hung should strain and break away. You would have thought that that little prisoner of the speckled head owned the tree, which in point of fact was owned by Temple Camp, notwithstanding its distance from the scout community. So it was really Hervey's more than it was little downy-head's if it comes to that.

It is not every landlord that goes to so much trouble for a tenant.

CHAPTER X

OFF WITH THE OLD LOVE, ON WITH THE NEW

"ALL right, we're coming down; kill the fatted calf," Hervey called with all his former gay manner. "No more up and down trails for me. This is moving day."

When he had descended a little nearer, Tom heard the cheery voice more clearly. "It's no easy job moving a house and family. I have to watch my step. Oh, boy, *coming down!* This tree is tied in a sailor's knot."

"Are you bringing the bird?" Tom called.

"I'm bringing the bird and the whole block he lived in," Hervey called back merrily. "I'm transplanting the neighborhood. He's going to move into a better locality—very fashionable. He's coming up in the world—I mean down.

O-o-h, boy, watch your step; there was a narrow escape! I stepped on a chunk of air."

So he came down working his way with both feet and one hand, and holding the precious piece of branch with its dangling nest in the other.

"Talk about your barbed wire entanglements," he called. Then, after a minute, "This little codger lives in a swing," he shouted; "I should think she'd get dizzy. No accounting for tastes, hey? Whoa—boy! There's where I nearly took a double-header. If I should fall now, I wouldn't have so far to go."

"You won't fall," said Tom with a note of admiring confidence in his brief remark.

"Better knock wood," came the cheery answer from above.

And presently his trim, agile form stood upon the lowest stalwart limb, as he balanced himself with one hand against the trunk. His khaki jacket was in shreds, a great rent was in his sleeve, and a tear in one of his stockings showed a long bloody scratch beneath. In his free hand he held the piece of branch with its depending nest, extending his arm out so as to keep the rescued trophy safe from any harm of contact.

"Some rags, hey?" he called down good-humoredly, and exposing his figure in grotesque attitude for sober Tom's amusement. "If mother could only see me now! Get out from under while I swing down. Back to terra cotta—I mean firma. Here goes——"

Down he came, tumbling forward, and sprawling on the ground, while he held the branch above him, like the Statue of Liberty lighting the world.

"Here we are," he said. "Take it while I have a look at my leg. It's nothing but an abrasion. It looks like a trail from my ankle up to the back of my knee. What care we? I've got trails on the brain, haven't I?"

Tom took the branch and stood looking admiringly, yet with a glint of amusement lighting his stolid features, at the younger boy, who sat with his knees drawn up humorously inspecting the scratch on his leg.

"Well, what do you think of eagles now?" Tom asked, in his dull way.

"Decline to be interviewed," Hervey said, with irrepressible buoyancy. "What kind of a crazy bird is this that lives upside down in a house that looks like a bat. It reminds me of a plum pudding, hanging in the pantry. What's that streak of red, anyway? His patrol colors? You'd think he'd get seasick, wouldn't you?"

"You've got the bird badge," Tom said, smiling a little; "can't you guess?"

What Tom did not realize was that this merry, reckless, impulsive young dare-devil, whose very talk, as he jumped from one theme to another, made him smile in spite of himself, could not be expected to bear in mind the record of his whole remarkable accomplishment. He was no hand-book scout.

There is the scout who learns a thing so that he may know it. But there is the scout who learns a thing so that he may do it. And having done it, he forgets it. Perhaps there is the scout who learns, does, and remembers. But Hervey was not of that order. He had made a plunge for each merit badge, won it and, presto, his nervous mind was on another. It takes all kinds of scouts to make a world.

Perhaps Hervey was not the ideal scout, but there was something very fascinating about his blithe way of going after a thing, getting it, and burdening his mind with it no more. He lived for the present. His naïve manner of asking Tom for a tip as to a trail had greatly amused the more experienced scout, who now could not understand how Hervey had used the handbook so much and knew it so imperfectly.

"Didn't you ever see one before?" Tom asked.

"Not while I was conscious," Hervey shot back, "but if he likes to live that way it's none of my business. He's inside taking a nap, I guess. He had some rocky road to Dublin coming down. I wonder what he thinks? That wasn't the right kind of a trail, was it?"

"Wasn't it?" Tom queried.

"No; I want a trail along the ground."

"Still after the Eagle, huh? Do you realize what you have done?"

"I've torn my suit all to shreds, I know that. Right the first time, hey? I'd look nice going up on the platform Saturday night? Good I won't have to, hey?"

"I thought you were going to," Tom said soberly.

"So I am," Hervey shot back at him; "trails up in the air don't count. Never mind, I'll find a trail to-morrow. It's my troop I'm thinking of.

I'll land it, all right.   When I get my mind on a thing. . . . Hey, Slady, what in the dickens is that streak of red in the nest?   Is it a trade mark or something like that?   You're a naturalist."

"It's an oriole's nest," Tom said, with just a note of good-humored impatience in his voice.   "I thought you'd know that."

"You see my head is full of the Eagle badge just now," Hervey pleaded, "but I'm going to look up orioles."

Tom smiled.

"I'm going to look up orioles, and I'm going to get Doc to put some iodine on my leg, and I'm going to do that tracking stunt to-morrow. There's three things I'm going to do."

Tom paused, seemingly irresolute, as if not knowing whether to say what was in his mind or not. And presently they started toward the camp, Hervey limping along and carrying the branch.

"An oriole picks up everything he can find and weaves it into his nest," Tom said; "string, ribbon, bits of straw, any old thing.   He likes things that are bright colored."

"He's got the right idea, there," Hervey said.

Tom tried again to interest the rescuer in this

little companion, imprisoned within its own cozy little home, whom they were taking back to camp. He could not comprehend how one who had performed such a stunt as Hervey had just performed, and been so careful and humane, could forget about his act so soon and take so little interest in the bird which had been saved by his reckless courage. But that was Hervey Willetts all over. His heart went where action was. And his interest lapsed when action ceased.

"Somebody in a book called the oriole Orestes, because that means dweller in the woods," Tom ventured.

"He dwells in a sky-scraper, that's what *I* say," Hervey commented. "In a hall bedroom upside down, twenty floors up."

Tom tried again. "What do you mean to do with her now that you've got her?" he asked.

"I'm going to turn her over to you, Slady. You're the real scout; none genuine unless marked T. S. You've got the birds all eating out of your hands."

"You didn't tear the nest from the branch," Tom said. "You must have had some idea."

"Well," said Hervey, "my idea was to stick it

up in an elm tree down at camp. Think she'd stand for it?"

"Guess so," Tom said.

"You see I'm all through bird study," Hervey said with amusing artlessness, "so I think you'd better adopt Erastus—is that the way you say it?"

"Orestes," Tom corrected him.

"Pardon *me*," Hervey said.

"Maybe you don't even care if I tell them what you did?" Tom queried.

"Tell them whatever you want," Hervey said. "I don't care. What I'm thinking now is——"

"The next stunt," Tom interrupted him.

"You said it," Hervey answered cheerily; "just about a mile or so of tracks. I guess you think I'm kind of happy-go-lucky, don't you?"

"I don't blame you for not remembering all the things you've done," Tom said, "and all the rules and tests and like that. But most every scout goes in for some particular thing. Maybe it's first aid, or maybe it's signaling. And he keeps on with that thing even after he has the badge."

"That's right," Hervey concurred with surprising readiness. "You've got the right idea. My specialty is the Eagle badge. See?"

"Well, that's twenty-one badges," Tom said.

"Right-o, and all I need to do now is test three for the stalking badge and I'm *it*. And if I can't go over the top between now and this time Saturday, I'll never look the fellows in my troop in the face again, that's what."

Tom whistled to himself a moment as they strolled along. Perhaps he knew more than he wished to say. Perhaps he was just a little out of patience with this sprightly, irresponsible young hero.

"Well, there isn't much time," he said.

"That's the trouble, Slady, and it's got me guessing."

CHAPTER XI

OFF ON A NEW TACK

It is doubtful if ever there was a scout at Temple Camp for whom Tom felt a greater interest or by whom he was more attracted than by this irrepressible boy whose ready prowess he had just witnessed. And the funny part of it was that no two persons could possibly have been more unlike than these two. Hervey even got on Tom's nerves somewhat by his blithe disregard of the handbook side of scouting, except for what it was worth to him in his stuntful career.

The handbook was almost a sacred volume to sober Tom. Still, he was captivated by Hervey, as indeed others were in the big camp.

"Well, you were after the Eagle and you got an oriole," he said, half jokingly. "That's what I meant when I said that sometimes you don't know where a trail will bring you out. You got a lot to learn about scouting. What you did to-day was better than tracking a half a mile or so."

"The pleasure is mine," said Hervey, in bantering acknowledgment of the compliment, "but if there's anything higher in scouting than the Eagle award, I'd like to know what it is."

"How much good has it done you trying for it?" Tom asked. "Nobody is supposed to go after a thing in scouting the same as he does in a game. He's supposed to learn things why he's going after something," he added in his clumsy way. "You went through the bird study test and you didn't even know it was an oriole's nest that you rescued. And you forgot all about something else too, and it makes me laugh when I think about it; when I think about you and your tracks."

"You think I'm a punk scout," Hervey sang out, gayly.

"I think you're a bully scout," Tom said.

"If I win the Eagle you'll say so, won't you?"

"Maybe."

"And do you mean to tell me that a scout can

up in a tree and I'll blow in later. I'm going on the war path for tracks. So long."

Before Tom had recovered from his surprise, Hervey was picking his way along the rocky ledge at the base of the mountain, apparently oblivious to all that had happened, and intent upon a rambling quest for tracks. It was quite characteristic of him that he based his search upon no hint or well considered plan, but went looking for the tracks of a wild animal as one will hunt for shells along the beach.

And there stood Tom, holding the memorial of Hervey's heroism in his hand. Hervey had apparently forgotten all about it. . . .

CHAPTER XII

AS LUCK WOULD HAVE IT

HERVEY picked his way among the rocks, looking here and there in the crevices and upon the
intervening ground as if he had lost something. A
more random quest could scarcely be imagined.
Tom watched him for a few minutes, then took the
shorter way to camp with his little charge.

Hervey followed the rocky ledge for about fifty
yards to a point where the dry bed of a stream
came winding down out of the mountain. It ran
in a tiny canyon between two rocks and so out
upon the level fields to the south where the camp
lay.

The twilight was well advanced now, the last
vivid patches were mellowed into a pervading gray,
which seemed to cover the rocks and woods like

a mantle. Clad in this somber robe, the wooded height which rose to the north seemed the more forbidding. Not a sound was to be heard but the voice of a whip-poor-will somewhere. Even Hervey's buoyant nature was subdued by the solemn stillness.

Suddenly something between the two rocks caught his eye. The caked earth looked as if a narrow board had been drawn over it. Bordering this broad line, about half an inch from it on either side, were two narrow fancy lines— or at least that is what Hervey called them. Examining these carefully, he saw that they were made up of tiny, diagonal lines. In the place where this ran between the rocks, in the deep shadow, these singular marks were surprisingly legible, and bore not a little the appearance of a border design. The big stones formed a sort of shadow box, causing the markings to appear in bold relief.

Hervey knew nothing of the freakish influence of light on tracks and trails, but he saw here something which he knew had been made by a moving object. The continuous design was so nearly perfect that it seemed like the work of human beings, but Hervey knew that it could hardly be this.

What, then, was it?

Where the lines emerged from between the rocks the marking was less regular and less clear, but plain enough in the damp, crusted earth which covered the mud in the old stream bed.

With heart bounding with joy and elation, Hervey followed the bed of the stream. The tracks, or whatever they were, were so clear that he could keep to the side of the muddy area and still see them.

It was characteristic of him that having made this great discovery, he did not trouble himself about the direction he was taking. In point of fact he was going in a southwesterly direction toward the camp.

For perhaps a quarter of a mile the strange markings were clearly legible in the dusk, running as they did in the yielding caked surface of the stream bed. They were as clear as tracks in caked snow. Then the path of the dried up waterway petered out in an area of rocks and pebbles and beyond that there was no clearly defined way; the brook had evidently trickled down into the lower land taking the path of least resistance among the rocks.

No doubt Tom Slade could have followed that water path to its end, but Hervey was puzzled, baffled. Yet the enthusiasm which carried him, as though on wings, to his triumphs was aroused now. He had the prophecy of Tom Slade to strengthen his determination. He must make good for Tom's sake now, as well as for the sake of his troop. He had told Tom that if he only once found a trail, nothing would stop him—*nothing*. Very fine. All that talk about there being something higher than the Eagle award was nonsense, and Tom Slade knew it was nonsense. "He said I'd do it, and I'm going to," Hervey muttered to himself.

Hervey had no patience with obstacles, he must be always moving, so now he began frantically scrutinizing the ground to see if he could find some sign of the marks which had eluded him. Since he could no longer distinguish the stream bed, he looked for some sign of those marks outside the stream bed.

And presently he was rewarded by the discovery of tracks, animal tracks sure enough, without any

ribbon, so to speak, printed between them. There
they were upon the hard, bare earth, two lines of
claw marks, continuing to a point where they disappeared again at the edge of a close cropped
field. Evidently his mysterious predecessor had
known just where he wished to go and had for-
saken the stream bed when it no longer went in his
direction. These were no aimless tracks, they
were the tracks of a creature that had particular
business in the southwest, and that knew how to
get there.

CHAPTER XIII

THE STRANGE TRACKS

HERVEY had not the slightest idea in which direction he was going, but in point of fact he was hitting straight in the direction of Temple Camp. But he had found his precious tracks and nothing would stop him now. He would go over the top in a blaze of glory next day, and then perhaps a telegram could be sent to scout headquarters to have the Eagle badge sent up immediately so that he could receive the very award itself on Saturday night. He was on the home stretch now, as luck would have it, and nothing would stop him—nothing. . . .

Nothing! He would send a line to his mother that very night and tell her all about it, and put E. S. after his name. *Eagle Scout.* The bicycle

his father had promised him when he should attain
that pinnacle of scout glory, he would now demand. That would be where dad lost out. . . .

If Tom Slade knew some secret about a higher
award, that meant more stunts, Hervey would do
those stunts, too; the more the merrier. He should
worry. . . .

Yes, he was on the trail at last, and at the end
of that trail was the stalking badge—and the
Eagle award. *Hervey Willetts, Eagle Scout.* It
sounded pretty good. . . .

He realized now that this discovery of his was
just a streak of luck, that the chances would have
been altogether against his finding real tracks in
these two remaining days. "I'm lucky," he said.
Which must have been true, else he would have
lost his life long ere that. . . .

Darkness was now coming on apace, and it must
be long past supper-time. But this was no time to
be thinking of eating. Nothing would stop him
now, *nothing*. When he set his mind on a
thing. . . .

The tracks changed again in traversing the
fields. They were not tracks at all, in fact, but a
narrow belt of trampled grass, which was not visi-

ble close by. It was only by looking ahead that
Hervey could distinguish it. Half way across the
field he lost it altogether, but, remembering the
fact that it could be seen better at a distance, he
climbed a tree and there lay the long narrow belt
of trampled grass running under the rail fence at
the field's edge and into the sparse woods beyond.
He had not to follow it, only pick out the rail of
the fence near where it passed and hurry to that
spot.

And there it was, waiting for him. If Hervey
had been well versed in tracking lore and less of
a seeker after glory, he would have scrutinized
the lowest rail of the fence, under which the track
went, for bits of hair. But Hervey Willetts was
not after bits of hair. It was quite like him that
he did not care two straws about what sort of
animal he was tracking. He was tracking the
Eagle badge.

In the sparse woods the tracks appeared as regular tracks again, sharply cut in the hard earth.
Where the ground was bare under the trees, the
tracks were as clear as writing on a slate, but in
the intervening spaces the vegetation obscured
them and he found them with difficulty. This

tracking in the woods was the hardest part of his task because it required patience and deliberation, and Hervey had neither.

But he managed it and was beginning to wonder how far his tracking had led him and whether he was near to covering the required distance. When he felt certain of that, he would drive a stake in the ground, fly his navy blue scarf from it to prove his claim, and go back to camp in triumph. He had made up his mind that he would at once report his feat in Council Shack, and offer to escort any or all of the trustees back over the ground in verification of his crowning accomplishment. The only Eagle Scout at Temple Camp, except Tom Slade; and Tom Slade didn't count. . . .

Still, as he looked back, the base of the mountain seemed almost as near as when he had made his discovery, the fields and wood which had seemed so long to the tracker were but small to the casual glance and he realized that his whole journey was yet far short of a quarter mile.

The tracks now ran, as clear as writing, across one of those curious patches of damp ground with a thin, slippery skin, which was torn straight across in a kind of furrow. Hervey was so intent on studying this that he did not notice in the shadow about a hundred feet ahead of him a log directly in line with the tracks. When suddenly he looked up, he paused and stared ahead of him in consternation.

Some one was sitting on the log.

CHAPTER XIV

HERVEY'S TRIUMPH

As soon as Hervey's dismay subsided he approached the log, and as he did so the figure appeared familiar to him. There was something especially familiar in the scout hat which came down over the ears of the little fellow who was underneath it, and in the hair which straggled out under the brim. The belt, drawn absurdly tight around the thin little waist, was a quite sufficient mark of identification. It was Skinny McCord, the latest find, and official mascot of the Bridgeboro troop, one of the crack troop of the camp. Alfred was his Christian name.

The queer little fellow's usually pale face looked ghastly white in the late dusk, and the strange brightness of his eyes, and his spindle legs and

72

diminutive body, crowned by the hat at least two sizes too large, made him seem a very elf of the woods. At camp or elsewhere, Skinny was always alone, but he seemed more lonely than ever in that still wood, with the night coming on. Nature was so big and Skinny was so little.

"Hello, Skinny, old top!" Hervey said cheerily. "What do you think you're doing here? Lost, strayed, or stolen?"

Skinny's eyes were bright with a strange light; he seemed not to hear his questioner. But Hervey, knowing the little fellow's queerness, was not surprised.

"You look kind of frightened.   Are you lost?" Hervey inquired.

For just a moment Skinny stared at him with a look so intense that Hervey was startled.   The little fellow's fingers which clutched a branch of the log, trembled visibly.   He seemed like one possessed.

"Don't get rattled, Skinny," Hervey said; "I'll take you back to camp. We'll find the way, all right-o."

"I'm a second-class scout," Skinny said.

"Bully for you, Skinny."

"I—I just did it. I'm going to do more so as to be sure. Will you stay with me so you can tell them? Because maybe they won't believe me."

"They'll believe you, Skinny, or I'll break their heads, one after another. What did you do, Alf, old boy?"

"Maybe they'll say I'm lying."

"Not while I'm around," Hervey said. "What's on your mind, Skinny?"

"I ain't through yet," Skinny said. "I know your name and I like you. I like you because you can dive fancy."

"Yes, and what are you doing here, Alf?" Hervey asked, sitting down beside the little fellow.

"I'm a second-class scout," Skinny said; "I found the tracks and I tracked them. See them? There they are. Those are tracks."

"Yes, I see them."

"I tracked them all the way up from camp and I've got to go further up yet, so as to be sure. You got to be *sure*—or you don't get the badge. So now I won't be a tenderfoot any more. Are you a second-class scout?"

"First-class, Skinny."

"I bet you don't care about tracks—do you?"

Hervey put his arm over the little fellow's shoulder and as he did so he felt the little body trembling with nervous excitement.

"Not so much, Skinny. No, I don't care about tracks. I—eh—I like diving better. How far up are you going to follow the tracks?"

"I'm going to follow them away, way, way up so as I'll be *sure*. They might say it wasn't a half a mile, hey?"

The hand which rested on the little thin shoulder, patted it reassuringly.

"Well, I'll be there to tell them different, won't I, Skinny, old boy?"

"Will you go with me all the way up to where the mountain begins—will you?"

"Surest thing you know."

"And will you prove it for me?"

"That's me."

"Then I won't be a tenderfoot any more. I'll be a second-class scout."

"Is that what you have to do to be a second-class scout, Skinny? I forget about the second-class tests. You have to track an animal, or something like that? I've got a rotten memory."

"And I'll—I'll have a trail named after me, too; it'll be called McCord trail. These are *my* tracks, see? Because I found them. Only maybe they'll say I'm lying. Anyway, how did *you* happen to come here?" he asked as if in sudden fear.

"I was just taking a walk through the woods, Skinny."

Skinny continued to stare at him, still with a kind of lingering misgiving, but feeling that gentle patting on his shoulder, he seemed reassured.

"I was just flopping around in the woods, Skinny; just flopping around, that's all. . . ."

CHAPTER XV

AND that was the triumph of Hervey Willetts, who would let nothing stand in his way. *"Nothing!"*

A hundred yards or so more and the stalking badge would have been won, and with it the Eagle award. The bicycle that he had longed for would have been his. The troop which in its confidence had commissioned him to win this high honor would have gone wild with joy. Hervey Willetts would have been the only Eagle Scout at Temple Camp save Tom Slade, and, of course, Tom didn't count.

Yet, strangely enough, the only eagle that Hervey Willetts thought of now was the eagle which he had driven off—the bird of prey. To have killed little Skinny's hope and dispelled his almost insane joy would have made Hervey Willetts feel just like that eagle which had aroused his wrath and reckless courage. "Not for mine," he muttered to himself. "Slady was right when he said he wasn't so stuck on eagles. He's a queer kind of a duck, Slady is; a kind of a mind reader. You never know just what he means or what he's thinking about. I can't make that fellow out at all. . . . I wonder what he meant when he said that a trail sometimes doesn't come out where you think it's going to come out. . . ."

Hervey had greatly admired Tom Slade, but he stood in awe of him now. "Well, anyway," said he to himself, "he said I'd win the award and I didn't; so I put one over on him." To put one over on Tom Slade was of itself something of a triumph. "He's not *always* right, anyway," Hervey reflected.

He was aroused from his reflections by little Skinny. "I followed them from camp," he said. "They're *real* tracks, ain't they? And they're *mine*, ain't they? Because I found them? Ain't they?"

"Bet your life. I tell you what you do, Alf, old boy. You just follow them up a little way further toward the mountain and I'll wait for you here. Then we can say you did it all by yourself, see? The handbook says a quarter of a mile or a half a mile, I don't know what, but you might as well give them good measure. I can't remember what's in the handbook half of the time."

"You know about good turns, don't you?"

" 'Fraid not, except when somebody reminds me."

"I'm going to keep you for my friend even if I *am* a second-class scout, I am," Skinny assured him.

"That's right, don't forget your old friends when you get up in the world."

"Maybe you'll get that canoe some day, hey?"

"What canoe is that, Alf?"

"The one for the highest honor; it's on exhibition in Council Shack. All the fellows go in to look at it. A big fellow let me go in with him, 'cause I'm scared to go in there alone."

"I haven't been inside Council Shack in three weeks," Hervey said. "I don't know what it looks like inside that shanty. I'm not strong on exhibitions. I'll take a squint at it when we go down."

"The highest honor, that's the Eagle award, isn't it?" Skinny asked.

"I suppose so," Hervey said; "a fellow can't get any higher than the top unless he has an airplane."

"Can he get higher than the top if he has a balloon?" Skinny wanted to know.

"Never you mind about balloons. What we're after now is the second-class scout badge, and we're going to get it if we have to kill a couple of councilmen."

"Did you ever kill a councilman?"

"No, but I will, if Alf McCord, second-class scout, doesn't get his badge. I feel just in the humor. Go on now, chase yourself up the line a ways and then come back. I'll be waiting at the garden gate."

"What gate?"

"I mean here on this log."

"Do you know Tom Slade?"

"You bet."

"He likes me, he does; because I used to steal things out of grocery stores just like he did— once."

"All right," Hervey laughed. "Go ahead now, it's getting late—Asbestos."

"That isn't my name."

"Well, you remind me of a friend of mine named Asbestos, and I remind myself of an eagle. Now don't ask any more questions, but beat it."

And so the scout who had never bothered his head about the more serious side of scouting sat on the log watching the little fellow as he followed those precious tracks a little further so that there might be no shadow of doubt about his fulfilling the requirement. Then Hervey shouted to him to come back, and shook hands with him and was the first to congratulate him on attaining to the dignity of second-class scout. Not a word did Hervey say about the amusing fact of little Skinny having followed the tracks backward; backward or forward, it made no difference; he had followed them, that was the main thing.

"They're *my* tracks; all mine," Skinny said.

"You bet," said Hervey; "you can roll them up and put them in your pocket if you want to."

Skinny gazed at his companion as if he didn't just see how he could do that.

And so they started down for camp together, verging away from the tracks of glory, so as to make a short cut.

"I bet you're smart, ain't you?" Skinny asked. "I bet you're the best scout in this camp. I bet you know everything in the handbook, don't you?"

"I wouldn't know the handbook if I met it in the street," Hervey said.

Skinny seemed a bit puzzled. "I had a bicycle that a big fellow gave me," he said, "but it broke. Did you ever have a bicycle?"

"Well, I had one but I lost it before I got it," Hervey said. "So I don't miss it much," he added.

"You sound as if you were kind of crazy," Skinny said.

"I'm crazy about you," Hervey laughed; and he gave Skinny a shove.

"Anyway, I like you a lot. And they'll surely let me be a second-class scout now, won't they?"

"I'd like to see them stop you."

CHAPTER XVI

IN DUTCH

THAT Hervey Willetts was a kind of odd number at camp was evidenced by his unfamiliarity with the things that were very familiar to most boys there. He was too restless to hang around the pavilion or sprawl under the trees or idle about with the others in and near Council Shack. He never read the bulletin board posted outside, and the inside was a place of so little interest to him that he had not even seen the beautiful canoe that was exhibited there, and on which so many longing eyes had feasted.

Now as he and Skinny entered that sanctum of the powers that were, he saw it for the first time. It was a beautiful canoe with a gold stripe around it and gunwales of solid mahogany. It lay on two sawhorses. Within it, arranged in tempting style, lay two shiny paddles, a caned back rest, and a handsome leather cushion. Upon it was a little typewritten sign which read:

This canoe to be given to the first scout this season to win the Eagle award.

"That's rubbing it in," said Hervey to himself. "That's two things, a bicycle and a canoe I've lost before I got them."

He sat down at the table in the public part of the office while Skinny, all excitement, stood by and watched him eagerly. He pulled a sheet of the camp stationery toward him and wrote upon it in his free, sprawling, reckless hand.

TO WHOM IT MAY CONCERN:

This will prove that Alfred McCord of Bridge-boro troop tracked some kind of an animal for more than a half a mile, because I saw him doing it and I saw the tracks and I came back with him and I know all about it and it was one good stunt I'll tell the world. So if that's all he's got to do to be a second-class scout, he's got the badge already, and if anybody wants to know anything about it they can ask me.

HERVEY WILLETTS,
Troop Cabin 13.

After scrawling this conclusive affidavit and placing it under a weight on the desk of Mr. Wade, resident trustee, Hervey sauntered over to the cabins occupied by the two patrols of his troop, the Leopards and the Panthers. They were just getting ready to go to supper.

"Anything doing, Hervey?" his scoutmaster, Mr. Warren, asked him.

"Nothing doing," Hervey answered laconically.

"Maybe he doesn't know what you're talking about," one of his patrol, the Panthers, suggested. This was intended as a sarcastic reference to Hervey's way of losing interest in his undertakings before they were completed.

"Have you got a trail—any tracks?" another asked.

Hervey began rummaging through his pockets and said, "I haven't got one with me."

"You didn't happen to see that canoe in Council Shack, did you?" Mr. Warren asked him.

"Yes, it's very nice," Hervey said.

Mr. Warren paused a moment, irresolute.

"Hervey," he finally said, "the boys think it's too bad that you should fall down just at the last minute. After all you've accomplished, it seems like—what shall I say—like Columbus turning back just before land was sighted."

"He didn't turn back," Hervey said; "now there's one thing I didn't forget—my little old history book. When Columbus started to cross the Delaware——"

"Listen, Hervey," Mr. Warren interrupted him; "suppose you and I walk together, I want to talk with you."

So they strolled together in the direction of the mess boards.

"Now, Hervey, my boy," said Mr. Warren, "I don't want you to be angry at what I say, but the boys are disgruntled and I think you can't blame them. They set their hearts on having the Eagle award in the troop and they elected you to bring it to them. I was the first to suggest you. I think we were all agreed that you had the, what shall I say, the pep and initiative to go out and get it. You won twenty badges with flying colors, I don't know how you did it, and now you're falling down all on account of *one single requirement.*

"Is that fair to the troop, Hervey? Is it fair to yourself? It isn't lack of ability; if it was I wouldn't speak of it. But it's because you tire of a thing before it's finished. Think of the things you learned in winning those twenty badges —the Morse Code, life saving, carpentry work. How many of those things do you remember now? You have forgotten them all—lost interest in them all. I said nothing because I knew you were after the Eagle badge with both hands and feet, but now you see you have tired of that—right on the threshold of victory. You can't blame the boys, Hervey, now can you?"

"Tracks are not so easy to find," Hervey said, somewhat subdued.

"They are certainly not easy to find if you don't look for them," Mr. Warren retorted, not un-pleasantly. "I heard a boy in camp say only this evening that that queer little duck in the Bridge-boro troop had found some tracks near the lake and started to follow them. There is no pair of eyes in camp better than yours, Hervey. But you know you can't expect to find animal tracks down in the village."

"In the village?"

"Two or three of your own patrol saw you down there a week ago, Hervey; saw you run out of a candy store to follow a runaway horse. You know, Hervey, horses' tracks aren't the kind you're after. Those boys were observant. They were on their way to the post office. I heard them telling Tom Slade about it."

"What did *he* say—Tom Slade?" Hervey queried.

"Oh, he didn't say anything; he never says much. But I think he likes you, Hervey, and he'll be disappointed."

"You think he will?"

"You know, Hervey, Tom Slade never won his place by jumping from one thing to another. The love of adventure and something new is good, but responsibility to one's troop, to oneself, is more important. How will your father feel about the bicycle he had looked forward to giving you? You see, Hervey, you regarded the winning of the Eagle award as an adventure, whereas the troop regarded it as a commission—a commission entailing responsibility."

"I'm not so stuck on eagles," said Hervey, repeating Tom Slade's very words. "There might be something better than the Eagle award, you can't tell."

"Oh, Hervey, my boy, don't talk like that, and

above all, don't let the boys hear you talk like that. There's nothing better than to finish what you begin—*nothing*. You know, Hervey, I understand you thoroughly. You're a wizard for stunts, but you're weak on responsibility. Now you've got some new stunt on your mind, and the troop doesn't count. Am I right?"

Hervey did not answer.

"And now the chance has nearly passed. Tomorrow we all go to the college regatta on the Hudson, the next day is camp clean-up and we've all got to work, and the next night, awards. Even if you were to do the unexpected now, I don't know whether we could get the matter through and passed on for Saturday night. I'm disappointed with you, Hervey, and so are the boys. We all expected to see Mr. Temple hand you the Eagle badge on Saturday night. I expected to send your father a wire. Walley has been planning to take our picture as an Eagle troop."

"Well, and you'll all be disappointed," said Hervey with a kind of heedlessness that nettled his scoutmaster. "And if anybody should ask you about it, any of the troop, you can just say that I found out something and that I'm not so stuck on the Eagle award, after all. That's what you can tell them."

"Well, I will tell them no such thing, for I would be ashamed to tell them that. I think we all know what the highest honor is. Perhaps the boys are not such reckless young adventurers as you, but they know what the highest scout honor is. And I think if you will be perfectly honest with me, Hervey, you'll acknowledge that something new has caught your fancy. Come now, isn't that right?"

"Right the first time," said Hervey with a gayety that quite disgusted his scoutmaster.

"Well, go your way, Hervey," he said coldly.

CHAPTER XVII

HERVEY GOES HIS WAY

So Hervey went his way alone, and a pretty lonesome way it was. The members of his troop made no secret of their disappointment and annoyance, he was clearly an outsider among them, and Mr. Warren treated him with frosty kindness. Hervey had been altogether too engrossed in his mad career of badge-getting to cultivate friends, he was always running on high, as the scouts of camp said, and though everybody liked him none had been intimate with him. He felt this now.

In those two intervening days between his adventure in the elm tree and the big pow-wow on Saturday night, he found a staunch friend in little Skinny, who followed him about like a dog. They stuck together on the bus ride down to the regatta on the Hudson and were close companions all through the day.

Hervey did not care greatly for the boat races, because he could not be in them; he had no use for a race unless he could win it. So he and Skinny fished for a while over the rail of the excursion boat, but Hervey soon tired of this, because the fish would not coöperate. Then they pitched ball on the deck, but the ball went overboard and Mr. Warren would not permit Hervey to dive in after it. So he made a wager with Skinny that he could shinny up the flag-pole, but was foiled in his attempt by the captain of the boat. Thus he was driven to the refuge of conversation.

Balancing himself perilously on the rail in an unfrequented part of the steamer, he asked Skinny about the coveted award. "They're not going to put you through a lot of book sprints, are they?" he inquired.

"I'm going to get it Saturday night," Skinny said. "I bet all my troop will like me then, won't they? I have to stand up straight when I go on the platform. Some fellows get a lot of clapping when they go on the platform. I know two fellows that are going to clap when I go on. Will you clap when I go on? Because I like you a lot."

"I'll stamp with both feet," said Hervey.

"And will you clap?"

"When you hear me clap you'll think it's a whole troop."

"I bet your troop think a lot of you."

"They could be arrested if they said out loud what they think of me."

"My father got arrested once."

"Well, I hope they won't trip you up. That was a fine stunt you did, Skinny. When those trustees and scoutmasters once get busy with the handbook, *good night,* it reminds you of boyhood's happy school days."

"It's all on page thirty," Skinny said; "and I've done all of those ten things, because the tracking made ten, and Mr. Elting said as long as you said you saw me do it, it's all right, because he knows you tell the truth."

"Well, that's one good thing about me," Hervey laughed.

"And he said you came near winning the Eagle award, too. He said you only just missed it. I bet you're a hero, ain't you?"

"Some hero."

"A boy said you gave the eagle a good run for it, even if you didn't get it. He said you came near it."

Hervey just sat on the rail swinging his legs. "I came pretty near the eagle, that's right," he said; "and if I'd got a little nearer I'd have choked his life out. That's how much I think of the eagle."

Skinny looked as if he did not understand.

"Did you see that bird that Tom Slade got? He got the nest and all. It's hanging in the elm tree near the pavilion. There's an oriole in that nest."

"Get out!"

"Didn't you see it yet?"

"Nope."

"All the fellows saw it. That bird has got a name like the one you called me."

"Asbestos?"

"Something like that. Why did you call me that name—Asbestos?"

"Well, because you're more important than an eagle.   See?"

"That's no good of a reason."

"Well, then, because you're going to be a second-hand scout."

"You mean second-*class*," Skinny said; "that's no good of a reason, either."

"Well, I guess I'm not much good on reasons. I'd never win the reason badge, hey?"

"Do you know who is the smartest fellow in this camp?" Skinny asked, jumping from one thing to another in his erratic fashion.   "Tom Slade. He knows everything.   I like him but I like you better.   He promised to clap when I go on the platform, too.   Will you ask your troop to clap?"

"I'm afraid they don't care anything about doing me a favor, Alf.   Maybe they won't feel like clapping.   But your troop will clap."

"Pee-wee Harris, he's in my troop; he said he'd shout."

"Good night!" Hervey laughed.   "What more do you want?"

CHAPTER XVIII

THE DAY BEFORE

So it seemed that Tom Slade had brought the rescued oriole, bag and baggage, back to camp, and had said nothing of the circumstance of his finding it. He was indeed a queer, uncommunicative fellow.

Surely, thought Hervey, this scout supreme could have no thought of personal triumphs, for he was out of the game where such things were concerned, being already the hero of scout heroes, living among them with a kind of romantic halo about his head.

Hervey was a little puzzled as to why Tom had not given him credit for finding that little stranger who was now a sort of mascot in the camp. For the whole scout family had taken very kindly to Orestes.

In the loneliness of the shadow under which he spent those two days, Hervey would have welcomed the slight glory which a word or two from Tom Slade might have brought him. But Tom Slade said nothing. And it was not in Hervey's nature to make any claims or boasts. He soon forgot the episode, as he forgot almost everything else that he had done and got through with. Glory for its own sake was nothing to him. He had climbed the tree and got his scout suit torn into shreds and that was satisfaction to him.

The next and last day before that momentous Saturday was camp clean-up day, for with the lake events on Labor Day the season would about close. All temporary stalking signs were taken down, original conveniences in and about the cabins were removed, troop and patrol fire clearings were raked over, two of the three large mess boards were stored away, and most of the litter cleared up generally. What was done in a small way each morning was done in a large way on this busy day, and every scout in camp did his share.

Hervey worked with his own troop, the members of which gave him scant attention. If they had ignored him altogether it would have been better than according him the cold politeness which they showed. No doubt their disappointment and humiliation were keen, and they showed it.

"What'll I do with this eagle flag?" one of them called, as he displayed an emblem with an eagle's head upon it, which one of the sisters of one of the boys had made in anticipation of the great event.

"Send it back to her," another shouted. "We ought to have a flag with a chicken's head on it. We counted our chickens before they were hatched."

"*Some* fall-down; we should worry," another said, busy at his tasks.

"Eagle fell asleep at the switch, didn't you, Eagle?"

They called him Eagle in a kind of ironical contempt, and it cut him more than anything else that they said.

"Eagle with clipped wings, hey?" one of the troop wits observed.

"Help us take down this troop pole, will you?" Will Connor, Hervey's patrol leader, called.

"We should bother about the eagle; our eagle isn't hatched yet."

"Some eggs are rotten," one of the Panthers retorted, which created a general laugh.

Hervey turned scarlet at this and his hands trembled on the oven stone which he was casting away. He dropped it and stood up straight, only to confront the stolid face of the young camp assistant looking straight at him.

"Getting all cleared up?" Tom asked in his usual sober but pleasant way.

Hervey Willetts was about to fly off the handle but something in Tom's quiet, keen glance deterred him.

"You fellows going home soon?"

"Tuesday morning," volunteered the Panthers' patrol leader. "We usually don't stick to the finish. We're a troop of quitters, you know."

"What did you quit?" asked Tom, taking his informant literally.

"Oh, never mind."

"It's all right, as long as you don't quit each other," Tom said, and strolled on to inspect the work of the other troops.

Hervey followed him and in a kind of reckless abandonment said, "Well, you see you were wrong after all—I don't care. You said I'd win it. So I put one over on you, anyway," he laughed in a way of mock triumph. "Tom Slade is wrong for once; how about that? The rotten egg put one over on you. See? I'm the rotten egg—the rotten egg scout. I should bother my head!"

"Go back and pick up those stones, Willetts," said Tom quietly, "and pile them up down by the woodshed."

"You didn't even tell them I saved that little bird, did you?" Hervey said, giving way to his feelings of recklessness and desperation. "What do you suppose *I* care? I don't care what anybody thinks. I do what I do when I do it; that's me! I don't care a hang about your old badges —I——"

"Hervey," said Tom; "go back and pile up those stones like I told you. And don't get mad at anybody. You do just what I tell you."

"Did you hear——"

"Yop. And I tell you to go back there and keep calm. I'm not interested in badges either;

I'm interested in scouts.   They'll never be able
to make a badge to fit you.   Now go back and do
what I told you.   Who's running this show?
You or I?"

CHAPTER XIX

THE GALA DAY

As long as the cheerful blaze near the lakeside gathers its scouts about it on summer evenings, Temple Camp will never forget that memorable Saturday night. It is the one subject on which the old scout always discourses to the new scout when he takes him about and shows him the sights.

The one twenty-two train from the city brought John Temple, founder of Temple Camp, sponsor of innumerable scout enterprises, owner of railroads, banks, and goodness knows what all. He was as rich as the blackberry pudding of which Pee-wee Harris (official cut-up of the Ravens) always ate three helpings at mess.

His coming was preceded by telegrams going in both directions, talks over the long distance 'phone, and when at last he came in all his glory, a rainbow troop consisting of honor scouts was formed to go down to Catskill Landing and greet him. One scout who would presently be handed the Gold Cross for life saving was among the number. Others were down for the Star Scout badge, and the silver and the bronze awards. Others had passed with peculiar distinction the many and difficult tests for first-class scout. One, a little fellow from the west, had won the camp award for signaling. There were others, too, with attainments less conspicuous and who were not in this gala troop, but the whole camp was out to honor its heroes, one and all.

Roy Blakeley, of the Silver Foxes, had a wooden rattle which he claimed could be heard for seven miles—eight miles and a quarter at a pinch. The Tigers, with Bert Winton at their head, had some kind of an original contrivance which simulated the roar of their ferocious namesake. The Church Mice, from down the Hudson, with Brent Gaylong as their scoutmaster, had a special squeal (patent applied for) which sounded as if all the mice in Christendom had gone suddenly mad. Pee-wee had his voice—enough said.

The Panthers and the Leopards, with Mr. Warren, watched the departure of this rainbow troop with wistful glances. Then the scoutmaster took his chagrined followers to their bare cabins, stripped of all that had made them comfortable and homelike in their long stay at camp. Hervey was not among them. No one in all the camp knew how he had suffered from homesickness in those two days. He wanted to be home—home with his mother and father.

To his disappointed troop Mr. Warren said:

Scouts, we have not won the coveted award. But in this fraternal community, every award is an honor to every scout. We will try to find pride in the achievements of our friends and camp comrades. Our mistake was in selecting for our standard bearer one whose temperament disqualified him for the particular mission which he undertook. No shortcoming of cowardice is his, at all events, and I blame myself that I did not suggest one of you older boys.

If we have not won the distinction we set our hearts on, our stay here has been pleasant and our achievement creditable, and for my part I give three cheers for the scouts who are to be honored and for the fortunate troops who will share their honors.

This good attempt to revive the spirits of his disappointed troop was followed by three feeble cheers, which ought to have gone on crutches, they were so weak.

Hervey was not in evidence throughout the day, and since no news is good news, one or two unquenchable spirits in his troop continued to hope that he would put in a dramatic appearance just in the nick of time, with the report of a sensational discovery—the tracks of a bear or a wild cat, for instance. It is significant that they would have been quite ready to believe him, whatever he had said.

But Mr. Warren knew, as his troop did not, of Hervey's saying that he wasn't so stuck on eagles, and he was satisfied from the talk that he had had with him that Hervey's erratic and fickle nature had asserted itself in the very moment of high responsibility. He could not help liking Hervey, but he would never again allow the cherished hopes of the troop to rest upon such shaky foundation.

Whatever lingering hopes the troop might have had of a last minute triumph were rudely dispelled when Hervey came sauntering into camp at about four o'clock twirling his hat on the end of a stick in an annoyingly care-free manner.

Tom Slade saw him passing Council Shack intent upon his acrobatic enterprise of tossing the hat into the air and catching it on his head, as if this clownish feat were the chief concern of his young life.

"You going to be on hand at five?" Tom queried in his usual off-hand manner.

"What's the use?" Hervey asked. "There's nothing in it for me."

Tom leaned against the railing of the porch, with his stolid, half interested air.

"Nothing in it for me," Hervey repeated, twirling his hat on the stick in fine bravado.

"So you've decided to be a quitter," Tom said, quietly.

Hervey winced a bit at this.

"You know you said you weren't so stuck on eagles," Hervey reminded him, rather irrelevantly.

"Well, I'm not so stuck on quitters either," Tom said.

"What's the good of my going? I'm not getting anything out of it."

"Neither am I," said Tom.

"You got stung when you made a prophecy

about me, didn't you?" Hervey said with cutting unkindness. "You and I both fell down, hey? We're punk scouts—we should bother our heads."

Again he began twirling his hat on the stick. "I couldn't sit with my troop, anyway," he added; "I'm in Dutch."

"Well, sit with mine, then; Roy Blakeley and that bunch are all from my home town; they're nice fellows. You know Pee-wee Harris—the little fellow that fell off the springboard?"

"I ought to like him; we both fell down."

"Well, you be on hand at five o'clock and don't make matters worse, like a young fool. If you've lost the eagle, you've lost it. That's no reason you should slight Mr. Temple, who founded this camp. We expect every scout in camp to be on hand. You're not the only one in camp who isn't getting the Eagle award."

"You call me a fool?"

"Yes, you're twenty different kinds of a fool."

"Almost an Eagle fool, hey?"

He went on up the hill toward his patrol cabin, tossing his hat in the air and trying to catch it on his head. As luck would have it, just before he entered the little rustic home of sorrow, the hat landed plunk on his head, a little to the back and very much to the side, and he let it remain in that rakish posture when he entered.

The effect was not pleasing to his comrades and scoutmaster.

CHAPTER XX

UNCLE JEB

At five o'clock every seat around the open air platform was occupied. Every bench out of Scout Chapel, the long boards on which the hungry multitude lined up at supper-time, every chair from Council Shack and Main Pavilion, and many a trunk and cedar chest from tents and cabins and a dozen other sorts of makeshift seating accommodations were laid under contribution for the gala occasion. And even these were not enough, for the whole neighboring village turned out in a body, and gaping summer boarders strolled into the camp in little groups, thankful for something to do and see.

There was plenty doing. Those who could not get seats sprawled under the trees in back of the seats and a few scouts perched up among the branches.

Upon the makeshift rustic platform sat the high dignitaries, scoutmasters, trustees—the faculty, as Hervey was fond of calling them. In the big chair of honor in the center sat Mr. John Temple and alongside him Commissioner Something-or-Other and Committeeman Something Else. They had come up from the big scout wigwam, in the dense woods on the corner of Broadway and Twenty-third Street, New York.

Resounding cheers arose and echoed from the hills when old Uncle Jeb Rushmore, retired ranchman and tracker, and scout manager of the big camp, took his seat among the high dignitaries. He made some concession to the occasion by wearing a necktie which was half way around his neck, and by laying aside his corn-cob pipe.

Tom Slade, who sat beside his superior, looked none the less romantic in the scout regalia which he wore in honor of the occasion. His popularity was attested as he took his seat by cries of "To-masso!" "Oh, you, Tomasso!" "Where did you get that scout suit, Tomasso?" "Oh, you, Tommy boy!"

Tom, stolid and with face all but expressionless, received these tributes with the faintest suggestion of a smile. "Don't forget to smile and look pretty!" came from the rear of the assemblage.

As was usual at Temple Camp festivities, the affair began with three resounding cheers for Uncle Jeb, followed by vociferous appeals for a speech. Uncle Jeb's speeches were an institution at camp. Slowly dragging himself to his feet, he sprawled over to the front of the platform and said in his drawling way:

"I don't know as thar's anything I got ter say. We've come out t'the end of our trail, en' next season I hope we'll see the same faces here. You ain't been a bad lot this year. I've seen wuss. I never seed a crowd that ate so much. I reckon none uv yer hez got homes and yer wuz all starved when yer come.

"Yer made more noise this season than anything I ever heard outside a Arizona cyclone. (Laughter) You've been noisy enough ter make a thunder-shower sound like a Indian lullaby. (Roars)

"If these here honor badges thet Mister Temple is goin' ter hand out'll keep yer quiet, I wish thar wuz more uv them. As the feller says, speech is silver and silence is gold, so I'm for gold awards every time. Onct I asked Buffalo Bill what wuz th' main thing fer a scout n' he says *silence*. (Uproarious laughter)' So I reckon th' best kind uv a boy scout is one that's deaf and dumb, but I ain't never seen none at this camp. I guess they don't make that kind.

"I wish yer all good luck and I congratulate you youngsters that are getting awards. If yer all got your just deserts——"

"I get three helpings," came a voice from somewhere in the audience. It was the voice of Peewee Harris. "I get *my* just desserts!"

Amid tumultuous cheering and laughter, old Uncle Jeb lounged back to his seat and Mr. John Temple arose.

CHAPTER XXI

THE FULL SALUTE

GREAT applause greeted Mr. Temple. He said:

"Gentlemen of our camp staff, visiting scoutmasters, and scouts:

"A friend of mine connected with the scout organization told me that he heard a scout say that Temple Camp without Uncle Jeb would be like strawberry short cake without any strawberries. (Great applause) I think that most scouts, including our young friend in back, would wish three helpings of Uncle Jeb. (Laughter)

"Coming from the bustling city, as I do, it is refreshing to see Uncle Jeb for I have never in all my life seen him in a hurry. (Laughter) All scouts can claim Uncle Jeb, he is the universal award that every boy scout wears in his heart. (Uproarious applause)

"Scouts, this is a gala day for me. It beats three helpings of dessert——"

"Sometimes we get four," the irrepressible voice shouted.

"I have been honored by the privilege of coming here to visit you in these quiet hills——"

A voice: "Sometimes it isn't so quiet."

"and to distribute the awards which your young heroes have earned. You can all be scouts; you cannot all be heroes. That is well, for as the old song says, 'When every one is somebody then no one's anybody.' (Laughter)

"I wonder how many of you scouts who are down for these awards realize what the awards mean? They are not simply prizes given for feats—or stunts, as you call them. To win a high honor merely as a stunt is to win it unfairly. Every step that a scout takes in the direction of a coveted honor should be a step in scouting. The Gold Cross is given *not* to one who saves life, but to a *scout* that saves life. Before you can win any honors in this great brotherhood, you must first be a scout. And that means that you must have the scout qualities.

"Scouting is no game to be won or lost, like baseball. After all, the high award is not for what you *do* alone, but for what you *are*. You are not to use scouting as a means to an end.

"In trying for a high award a scout is not running a race with other scouts. There is no spirit of contest in scouting. To be a hero, even that is not enough. One must be a *scout* hero. He must not use the animals and birds and the woods to help in his quest of glory, whether it be troop glory or individual glory. He must not ask the birds and animals to tell him their secrets simply that he may win a piece of silver or gold to hang on his coat. But he must learn to be a friend to the birds and animals. For that is true scouting.

"You will notice that on the scout stationery is printed our good motto, *Do a good turn daily.* There is nothing there about high awards. Evidently the good turn daily is considered of chief importance. Nothing can supersede that. It stands above and apart from all awards. Kindness, brotherliness, helpfulness—there is no metal precious enough to make a badge for these."

As Mr. Temple turned to take the first award from Mr. Wade the assemblage broke into wild applause. Perhaps Mr. Warren, sitting among his disappointed troop, hoped that Mr. Temple's words would be taken to heart by the absent member. But none of the troop made any comment.

After the distribution of a dozen or so merit badges, Mr. Temple called out, "Alfred McCord, Elk Patrol, First Bridgeboro, New Jersey Troop."

There was a slight bustle among the Bridgeboro boys to make way for their little member who started threading his way among the throng, his thin little face lighted with a nervous smile of utter delight.

"Bully for Alf!" some one called.

"Greetings, Shorty," another shouted.

He stood before Mr. Temple on the platform, trembling all over, and yet the picture of joy. His big eyes stared with a kind of exaltation. For once, his hair was smooth, and it made his face seem all the more gaunt and pale. This was the crucial moment of his life. He stood as straight as he could, his little spindle legs shaking, but his hand held up in the full scout salute to Mr. Temple. Oh, but he was proud and happy. If Hervey Willetts, wherever he was, saw him one brief thrill of pride and satisfaction must have been his.

"Alfred McCord," said Mr. Temple; "your friends and I greet you as a scout of the second-class. Let me place on you the symbol of your achievement."

He stepped forward, just one step. Oh, but he was happy. He stood upon the platform, but he walked on air. Mr. Temple shook hands with him—Mr. John Temple, founder of Temple Camp! Yes, sir, Skinny and Mr. John Temple shook hands. And then the little fellow turned so that the audience might see his precious badge. And the wrinkles at the ends of his thin little

mouth showed very clearly as he smiled—oh, such
a smile.

Then the scouts of Temple Camp showed that
their wonted disregard of Skinny was only because they did not understand him, queer little
imp that he was. For cheer after cheer arose
as he stood there in a kind of bewilderment of
joy.

"Hurrah, for the star tracker!"

"Three cheers for the sleuth of the forest!"

"No more tenderfoot!"

"Hurrah for S-S-S!" Which meant Skinny,
second-class scout.

"I congratulate you, Alfred," said Mr. Temple, pleased at the ovation. "You have the
eyes that see, and this feat of tracking which
I have heard of is a fitting climax to all your
efforts to win your goal—to finish what you began.
Let every tenderfoot follow your example. And
may the scouts of the second-class welcome you
with pride."

Skinny saw Mr. Temple's hand raised, saw the
fingers formed to make the familiar scout salute
—the *full* salute. The full salute for him! He

saw this and yet he did not see it; he saw it in a kind of daze.

Then he went down and stepped upon the earth again and made his way back to his seat. Those who saw him thought that he was walking, but he was not walking, he was floating on wings. And the noise about and the big trees in back, and the faces that smiled at him as he passed, were as things seen and heard in a dream. . . .

CHAPTER XXII

TOM RUNS THE SHOW

"WILLIAM CONWAY, Anson Jenks, and George Winters, for Star Scout badge, and Merritt Roth and Edward Collins for bronze life saving medals. These scouts will please step forward."

Amid great applause they made their way to the platform and one by one returned, greeted with cheers.

"Gaynor Morrison of Edgemere Troop, Connecticut, is awarded the Gold Cross for saving life at imminent hazard of his own. Congratulations to him but more to his troop. Scout Morrison will please come forward."

That was the moment of pride for Edgemere Troop, Connecticut. Gaynor Morrison, tall and muscular, stood before Mr. Temple and listened to such plaudits as one seldom hears in his own honor. He went down overjoyed and blushing scarlet.

"And now," said Mr. Temple, "the last award is properly not an organization award at all. It is the Temple Camp medal for order and cleanliness in and about troop cabins. It is awarded to Willis Norton of the Second Oakdale, New Jersey, Troop. And that, I think, concludes this pleasant task of distributing honors. I think you will all be glad to know that one who is a stranger to no honor wishes himself to say a few words to you now. Whatever Tom Slade may have to say goes with me——"

He could not say more. Cries of "Bully old Tom!" "Hurrah for Tomasso!" "What's the matter with old Hickory Nut?" "Oh, you, Tom Slade," "Spooch, spooch!" "Hear, hear!" arose from every corner of the assemblage and the cries were drowned in a very tempest of applause.

He never looked more stolid, nor his face more expressionless than when he arose from his chair. He was neither embarrassed nor elated. If he was at all swayed by the sudden tribute, it was as an oak tree might be swayed in a summer breeze. He knew what he wanted to say and he

MR TEMPLE CONGRATULATES HERVEY WILLETTS.

Tom Slade on Mystery Trail.   *Page* 124

was going to say it. He waited, he *had* to wait, for at least five minutes, till Temple Camp had had its say.

Then he said, slowly, deliberately, with a kind of mixture of clumsiness and assurance which was characteristic of him.

"Maybe I haven't got any right to speak. I'm not on the staff, and as you might say, I'm through being a scout——"

"Never, Tomasso!" said a voice.

"But I saw something that none of you saw and I know something that none of you know about—except Mr. Temple, that I told it to, and the trustees.

"Since I been assistant to Uncle Jeb—that's two years—I saw the Eagle award given out twice——"

"You won it yourself, Tomasso!"

"I saw it given to a scout from Virginia and one from New York. You always hear a lot of talk about the Eagle award here in camp. Lots of scouts start out big and don't get away with it. I guess everybody knows it isn't easy. If you're an Eagle Scout you're everything else. You got to be.

"I've seen scouts get it. But in the last couple of days I saw one chuck it in the dirt and trample on it. That's because when a fellow gets so far that he's really an Eagle Scout, he doesn't care so much about it. A fellow's got to be a scout to win the Eagle badge. And if he's enough of a scout for that, he's enough of a scout to give it up if there's any reason. What does *he* care? If he's scout enough to be an Eagle Scout, and gives it up, he doesn't even bother to tell anybody. Being willing to give it up is part of winning it, as you might say.

"Maybe you people didn't know who you were cheering when you cheered Alfred McCord. But I'll tell you who you were cheering. You were cheering the only Eagle Scout in Temple Camp. And he doesn't care any more about the Eagle badge than he does about what every little tin scout in his own troop thinks of him, either. And I'm standing here to tell you that. I saw that scout give up one badge and win another at the same time. I saw him lose the stalking badge and win the animal first aid badge all inside of an hour. He thought he lost out by giving up his tracks to Alfred McCord, when he might have scared the life out of the little fellow and chased him back to camp.

"But all the time he had an extra badge and he didn't know it. That's because he doesn't bother about the handbook and because he wins badges so fast he can't keep track of them. He's an Eagle Scout and he doesn't know it. He threw one badge away and caught another and he's coming up here now to stand still for two minutes if he can and listen to the paper that Mr. Temple is going to read to him. Come ahead up, Hervey Willetts, or I'll come down there and pull you out of that tree and drag you up by the collar!"

CHAPTER XXIII

PEE-WEE SETTLES IT

FOR half a minute there was no response, and the people, somewhat bewildered, stared here and there, applauding fitfully.

"Come ahead, I know where you are," Tom pronounced grimly; "I'll give you ten seconds."

The victim knew that voice; perhaps it was the only voice at camp which he would have obeyed. There was the sound of a cracking branch, followed by a frightened cry of "Look out!" Some one called, "He'll kill himself!" Then a rustling of leaves was heard, and down out of the tree he came and scrambled to his feet, amid cries of astonishment. Hervey Willetts was running true to form and the moment of his triumph was celebrated by a new stunt.

"Never mind brushing off your clothes," said Tom grimly; "come up just the way you are."

But he did not go up the steps, not he. He vaulted up onto the platform and stood there brushing the dirt from his torn khaki suit. The crowd, knowing but yet only half the story of his triumph, was attracted by his vagabond appearance, and his sprightly air. The rent in his sleeve, his disheveled hair, and even the gaping hole in his stocking seemed to be a part of him, and to bespeak his happy-go-lucky nature. As he stood there amid a shower of impulsive applause, he stooped and hoisted up one stocking which seemed in danger of making complete descent, and that was too much for the crowd.

Even Mr. Temple smiled as he said, "Come over here, my young friend, and let me congratulate the only Eagle Scout at Temple Camp."

And so it befell that Hervey Willetts found himself clasping in cordial grip the friendly hand of Mr. John Temple with one hand while he still hauled up his rebellious stocking with the other. It was a sight to delight the heart of a movie camera man. His stocking was apparently the only thing that Hervey could not triumph over.

"My boy," said Mr. Temple, "it appears that we know more about you than you know about yourself. It appears that your memory and your handbook study have not kept pace with your sprightly legs and arms——"

"How about his dirty face?" some one called.

"And his stocking?" another shouted.

"These are the honorable scars of war," Mr. Temple said, "and I think I prefer his face as it is. I think we shall have to take Hervey Willetts as we find him, and be satisfied.

"Hervey Willetts," he continued, "you stand here to-day the easy winner of the greatest honor it has ever been my pleasure to confer. Stand up, my boy, and never mind your stocking. (Laughter.) You have won the Eagle award, and you have made your triumph beautiful and unique by working into it one of the best good turns in all the history of scouting. I doubt whether a youngster of your temperament can ever really appreciate what you have done. But of course you could not escape Tom Slade—no one could. He has your number, as boys say——"

"Bully for Tom Slade!" a voice called.

"What's the matter with Tomasso?"

"Hurrah for old Sherlock Nobody Holmes!"

"Oh, you, Tommy!"

"Tag, you're it, Hervey!"

"I have here a paper procured by Tom Slade," Mr. Temple continued, "and bearing the signatures of three scouts—John Weston, Harry Bonner and George Wentworth. These scouts testify that they were in Catskill village drinking soda water——"

"That's all they ever go there for," a voice shouted.

"They saw Hervey Willetts stop a runaway horse, saw him unfasten the harness of the animal when it fell, frightened and exhausted, and saw him procure and pour cool water on the animal's head. This was never reported in camp till Tom Slade made inquiries. Hervey Willetts had neglected to report it."

"He's a punk scout," some one called.

"I have here also," Mr. Temple continued, "the testimony of Tom Slade himself that Hervey Willetts climbed a tree and in a daring manner saved a bird and its nest from the ruthless assault of an eagle. That bird's nest, with its little occupant, hangs now in the elm tree at the corner of the pavilion." (Great applause.)

"Thus Hervey Willetts won the animal first aid badge without so much as knowing it. (Applause.) He had won twenty-one merit badges and he did not know it. (Great applause.) He was then and there an Eagle Scout and he did not know it. (Deafening cheers.) But Tom Slade knew it and said nothing——"

"Thomas the Silent," some irreverent voice called.

"So you see, my friends, it really made no difference whether our young hero tracked an animal or not. He was an Eagle Scout. He could go no higher. He had reached the pinnacle—no, not quite that. To his triumph he must add the glory of a noble, unselfish deed. Never knowing that the coveted honor was already his, he set out to win it by a tracking stunt which would fulfill the third requirement to bring him the stalking badge, and with it the Eagle award. He had said that nothing would stand in his way, not even mountains. He had made this boast to Tom Slade.

"And that boast he failed to make good. Something *did* stand in his way. Not a mountain. Just a little tenderfoot scout. You have seen him up here. Alfred McCord is his name. (Applause.)

"And when Hervey Willetts found this little scout hot upon the trail, he forgot about the Eagle award, forgot about his near triumph, braved the anger and disappointment of his friends and comrades——"

The troop of which Hervey was a member arose in a sudden, impetuous burst of cheering, but Mr. Temple cut them short.

"Just a moment and then you may have your way. Hervey Willetts cared no more about the opinion of you scouts than this big oak tree over my head cares about the summer breeze. There were two trails there, one visible, the other invisible. One on the ground, the other in his heart. And Hervey Willetts was a scout and he hit the right trail. If it were not for our young assistant camp manager here, Hervey Willetts would this minute be witnessing these festivities from yonder tree, and little would he have cared, I think.

"But he reckoned without his host, as they say,

when he sought the aid of Tom Slade.   (Deafening applause.)   Tom Slade knew him even if he did not know himself.

"My friends, many scouts have sought the Eagle award and a few have won it.   But the Eagle award now seeks Hervey Willetts.   He threw it aside but still it comes to him and asks for acceptance.   He deserves something better, but there is nothing better which we have to give. For there is no badge for a noble good turn. Tom Slade was right."

"You said something!" some one shouted.

"To be enough of a scout to win the Eagle award is much.   To be scout enough to ignore it is more.   But twenty-one badges is twenty-one badges, and the animal first aid badge is as good as any other.   The technical question of whether a bird is an animal——"

"Sure a bird's an animal!" called a voice from a far corner which sounded suspiciously like the voice of Pee-wee Harris.   "Everybody's an animal—even I'm an animal—even you're an animal —sure a bird's an animal!   That's not a teckinality!   Sure a bird's an animal!"

"Well, then, that settles it," laughed Mr. Tem-

ple amid a very tempest of laughter, "if that is
Mr. Harris of my own home town speaking, we
have the opinion of the highest legal expert on
scouting——"

"And eating!" came a voice.

Thus, amid an uproarious medley of laughter
and applause, and of cheering which echoed from
the darkening hills across the quiet lake, Hervey Willetts stood erect while Mr. John Temple,
founder of the camp and famous in scouting cir-
cles the world over, placed upon his jacket the
badge which made him an Eagle Scout and inci-
dentally brought him the canoe on which so many
eyes had gazed longingly.

And then one after another, pell-mell, scouts
clambered onto the platform and surrounded him,
while the scouts of his own troop edged them aside
and elbowed their way to where he stood and
mobbed him.   And amid all this a small form,
with clothing disarranged from close contact, but
intent upon his purpose, squirmed and wriggled
in and threw his little skinny arms around the
hero's waist.

"Will you—will you take me out in it?" he
asked.   "Just once—will you?"

"The canoe?" Hervey said.   "You'll have to ask my troop, Alf, old top; it belongs to them. What would a happy-go-lucky nut like I am be doing, paddling around in a swell canoe like that?"

"Let me—let me see the badge," little Skinny insisted.

But already Hervey had handed the badge over to his troop.   Probably he thought that it would interfere with his climbing trees or perhaps fall off when he was hanging upside down from some treacherous limb or scrambling head foremost down some dizzy cliff.   No doubt it would be more or less in the way during his stuntful career. . . .

CHAPTER XXIV

THE RED STREAK

THERE was one resident at Temple Camp who did not attend that memorable meeting by reason of being sound asleep at the time. This was Orestes, the oriole, who had had such a narrow squeak of it up at the foot of the mountain. Orestes always went to bed early and got up early, being in all ways a model scout.

It is true that just at the moment when the cheering became tumultuous, Orestes shook out her feathers and peered out of the little door of her hanging nest but, seeing no near-by peril, settled down again to sweet slumber, never dreaming that the cheering was in honor of her scout rescuer.

The housing problem did not trouble Orestes

much. One tree was as good as another so long as her architectural handiwork was not desecrated, and having once satisfied herself that her little home still depended from the very branch which she had chosen, she did not inquire too particularly into the facts of that magic transfer. The branch rested across two other branches and Orestes was satisfied.

That was a happy thought of Tom's to call the oriole Orestes, which means dweller in the woods, but thanks to Hervey the name became corrupted in camp talk, and the nickname of Asbestos caught the community and became instantly popular.

The shady area under Asbestos' tree was already a favorite lounging place for scouts, and lying on their backs with knees drawn up (a favorite attitude of lounging) they could see that mysterious little red streak in their little friend's nest. In the late afternoon, which was ever the time of sprawling, the sun had a way of poking one of his rays right down through the dense foliage plunk on Asbestos' nest, and then the little red streak shone like Brick Warner's red hair after he had been diving. But no one ventured up to that little home to investigate that freakish streak of color.

"I'd like to know what that is?" Pee-wee Harris observed as he lay on his back, peering up among the branches.

Half a dozen scouts, including Roy Blakeley and Hervey Willetts, were sprawling under the tree waiting for supper, on the second afternoon after Hervey's triumph. Waiting for supper was the favorite outdoor sport at Temple Camp. Orestes was already tucked away in bed, having dined early on three grasshoppers and an angleworm for dessert.

"That's easy," said Roy Blakeley; "Asbestos is a red—she's an anarchist. We ought to notify the government."

"Asbestos is an I.W.W. He ought to be deported," Hervey said.

"He's a *she*," Pee-wee said.

"Just the same I'd like to know what that red streak really does mean," Roy confessed.

"It's better than a yellow streak anyway," Hervey laughed; "maybe it's her patrol color."

"That's a funny thing about an oriole," another scout observed; "an oriole picks up everything it sees, string and ribbon and everything like that, and weaves it into its nest."

"They should worry about building material," Roy said.

"I read about one that got hold of a piece of tape and weaved it in," said the scout who had volunteered the information. Maybe that's tape."

"Sure, she ought to work for the government, there's so much red tape about her," Roy observed.

"It's the color of cinnamor taffy," Pee-wee said.

"There you go on eats again," Roy retorted; "it's the color of pie."

"What kind of pie?" Pee-wee asked.

"Any kind," Roy said; "take your pick."

"You're crazy," Pee-wee retorted.

Their idle banter was interrupted by Westy Martin of Roy's and Pee-wee's troop who paused at the tree as they returned from the village. Westy was waving a newspaper triumphantly.

"What do you know about this?" he said, opening the paper so that the scouts could see a certain heading.

"Oh, me, oh, my!" Roy said. "Isn't Temple Camp getting famous? Talk about *red!* Oh, boy, watch Hervey's beautiful complexion when he hears this. He'll have cinnamon taffy beat a mile."

Willy-nilly, Roy snatched the news sheet from Westy and read:

TEMPLE CAMP HAS NEW HERO

Yesterday was a gala day up at the scout camp. More than five hundred people from hereabouts, as well as the whole population of the famous scout community, cheered themselves hoarse when Mr. John Temple, founder of the big camp, distributed the awards for the season.

For the first time in four years Temple Camp produced an Eagle Scout in Hervey Willetts of a Massachusetts troop who won the award under circumstances reflecting unusual credit on himself and bringing honor to his troop comrades. Mr. Temple's remarks to this young hero were flattening in the last degree——

"You mean flattering," Pee-wee shouted.

"Excuse myself," said Roy.

and it was decided to give Hervey the award, because Scout Harris proved excruciatingly—I mean exclusively—I mean conclusively—that a bird is an animal just the same as Mr. Temple is, only different——

"Let me see that!" shouted Pee-wee. "You make me sick! Where is it?"

"Here's something to interest you more," Roy said; "here's the real stuff—a kidnapping. A kid was taking a nap and got kidded."

"Where?" Pee-wee demanded.

"There," Roy said, pointing triumphantly to a heading which put the Temple Camp notice in the shade. "Just read that."

But for that sensational article, doubtless Hervey would have been more of a newspaper hero instead of being stuck down in a corner. The article was indeed one to arouse interest and call for big headings, and the scouts, gathered about Roy, peered over his shoulders and read it eagerly.

MILLIONAIRE HARRINGTON'S SON
KIDNAPPED

Alarm Sent Out for Child Missing More Than Week

TRAIN HAND GIVES CLEW

Police authorities throughout the country have been asked to search for Anthony Harrington, Jr., the little son of Anthony Harrington, banker, of

New York. The child, aged about ten, disappeared about a week ago and since then an exhaustive search privately made has failed to yield any clew of the little fellow's whereabouts.

When last seen the child was playing on the lawn of his father's beautiful estate at Irvington-on-Hudson on Friday a week ago. From that time no trace of him has been discovered.

The only bit of information suggesting a possible clew comes from Walter Hanlon, a trainman who told the authorities yesterday that on an afternoon about a week ago his attention was drawn to a child accompanied by two men leaving his train at Catskill Landing. Hanlon's train was northbound. He reported what he had seen as soon as the public alarm was given.

Hanlon said that he noticed the child, a boy, as he helped the little fellow down the car steps, because of an open jack-knife which the youngster carried, and which he good-naturedly advised him to close before he stumbled with it. To the best of Hanlon's recollection the little fellow wore a mackinaw jacket, but he did not notice this in particular. It is known that the child wore a sweater when he disappeared.

Hanlon paid no attention to the child's companions and his recollection of their appearance is hazy. He says that the three disappeared in the crowd and he thought they joined the throng which was waiting for the northbound boat of the Hudson River Day Line. If such was the case, the authorities believe that the party left the train and continued northward by boat in hopes of baffling the authorities.

One circumstance which lends considerable color

to Hanlon's statement is the positive assurance of the child's parents that their son had no jack-knife of any description. This, therefore, may mean that the child was not the Harrington child at all, or on the other hand, it may mean, what seems likely, that the men gave the little fellow a jack-knife as a bribe to accompany them. Hanlon thinks that the knife was new, and is sure that the child was very proud of it.

So much of this sensational article was in conspicuous type. The rest, in regulation type, pertained to the unsuccessful search for the child by private means. A couple of ponds had been dragged, the numerous acres of the fine estate had been searched inch by inch, barns and haystacks and garages and smokehouses had been ransacked, an old disused well had been explored, the neighboring woodland had been covered, but little Anthony Harrington, Jr., had disappeared as completely as if he had gone up in the clouds.

"You fellows had better be getting ready for supper," said Tom Slade, as he passed.

"Look here, Tomasso," said Roy.

Tom paused, half interested, and read the article without comment.

"Some excitement, hey?" said Roy.

"It's a wonder they didn't mention the color of

the sweater while they were about it," Tom said.

"The kid had on a mackinaw jacket," Roy shot back.

"How do we know what was under the mackinaw jacket?" Tom said. "Come on, you fellows, and get washed up for grub."

"Mm-mmm," said Pee-wee Harris.

CHAPTER XXV

THE PATH OF GLORY

THE affair of the kidnapping created quite a sensation at camp, partly, no doubt, because stories of missing people always arouse the interest of scouts, but chiefly perhaps because the thing was brought so close to them.

Catskill Landing was the station for Temple Camp. It was there that arriving troops alighted from boat or train. It was the frequent destination of their hikes. It was there that they bought sodas and ice cream cones. Scouts from "up ter camp" were familiar sights at Catskill, and they overran the village in the summertime.

Of course it was only by reason of trainman Hanlon's doubtful clew that the village figured at all in the sensational affair. At all events if the

Harrington child and its desperate companions had actually alighted there, all trace of them was lost at that point.

The next morning after the newspaper accounts were published a group of scouts hiked down to Catskill to look over the ground, hoping to root out some information or discover some fresh clew. They wound up in Warner's Drug Store and had a round of ice cream sodas and that was all the good their sleuthing did them.

On the way back they propounded various ingenious theories of the escape and whereabouts of Master Harrington's captors. Pee-wee Harris suggested that they probably waited somewhere till dark and proceeded to parts unknown in an airplane. A more plausible inspiration was that they had crossed the Hudson in a boat in order to baffle the authorities and proceeded either southward to New York or northward on a New York Central train.

The likeliest theory was that of Westy Martin of Roy's troop, that an automobile with confederates had waited for the party at Catskill. That would insure privacy for the balance of the journey.

The theory of one scout that the party had gone aboard a cabin cruiser was tenable, and this means of hiding and confounding the searchers, seemed likely to succeed. The general opinion was that ere long the child would be forthcoming in response to a stupendous ransom. But this means of recovering the little fellow did not appeal to the scouts.

Perhaps if Tom Slade, alias Sherlock Nobody Holmes, had accompanied the group down to the riverside village, he would have learned or discovered something which they missed. But Sherlock Nobody Holmes had other business on hand that morning.

"Do you want to see it? Do you want to see it?" little Skinny had asked him. "Do you want to see those tracks I found? Do you want to see me follow them again? Do you want to see how I did it—do you?" And Tom had given Skinny to understand that it was the dream of his life to see those famous tracks, which had proved a path of glory to the golden gates which opened into the exalted second-class of scouting.

"I'll show them to you! I'll show them to you!" Skinny had said eagerly. "I'll show you where I began. Maybe if we wait till it rains they'll get not to be there any more maybe."

So Tom went with him to the rock close by the lake shore where the path to glory began, and starting here, they followed the tracks, now becoming somewhat obscure, up into the woods.

"Before I started I made sure," Skinny panted, as he trotted proudly along beside his famous companion. "The scouts they said you'd be too busy to go with me, they did. But you ain't, are you?"

"That's what," said Tom.

"I bet you don't shake all over when Mr. Temple speaks to you, do you?"

"Not so you'd notice it."

"I bet he's got as much as a hundred dollars, hasn't he?"

"You said it."

"Maybe if I wasn't a-scared I'd ask him to look at the tracks too, hey? First off I was a-scared to ask *you?*"

"Tracks are my middle name, Alf."

"Now I can prove I'm a second-class scout by my badge, can't I?"

"That's what you can. But you've got it pinned

on the wrong side, Alf. Here, let me fix it for you."

"Everybody'll be sure to see it, won't they?"

"That's what they will."

"Hervey Willetts, he's a hero, isn't he?"

"You bet."

"I'd like to be like him, I would."

"He's kind of reckless, Alf. It's bad to be too reckless."

"I wouldn't let you talk against him—I wouldn't."

Tom smiled. "That's right, Alf, you stand up for him."

"Maybe you don't know what kind of an animal made these tracks, maybe, hey?"

Indeed Tom did not know. But one thing he knew which amused him greatly. They were following the path of glory the wrong way. Not that it made any particular difference, but it seemed so like Skinny. He had not actually tracked an animal at all, since the animal had come toward the lake. He had followed tracks, to be sure, but he had not tracked an animal. Hervey must have known this but he had not mentioned it. The thought thrilled even stolid Tom with fresh admiration for that young adventurer. Hervey Willetts was no handbook scout, but Tom would not have him different than he was—no, not by a hair. He thought how Skinny's beginning at the wrong end was like his pinning of the badge on the wrong side of his breast. Poor little Skinny. . . .

And he thought of that other scout coming down through those woods, tracking that mysterious animal indeed, and stopping short, and sitting down on a log and throwing away his triumph like chaff before the wind. Then there arose in his mind the picture of that bright-eyed, irresponsible youngster with his hat cocked sideways on his head, off upon some new adventure or bent on some new stunt. Not a very good scout delegate perhaps, but the bulliest scout that ever tore a gaping hole in his stocking. . . .

Tom was aroused from his meditation by Skinny's eager voice. "Here's the log where he talked to me," he said; "here's just the very same place we sat down and he said he'd be my witness. He said I was old top, that's what he called me."

"Old top, hey?" said Tom, smiling.

CHAPTER XXVI

MYSTERIOUS MARKS

BEFORE reaching the log, Tom's interest had been chiefly in his queer little companion. The tracks puzzled him somewhat, but since they had already served their purpose and were in process of obliteration he paid little attention to them. In his more ambitious rambles during late fall and winter, he had run across too many tracks of deer and bear and wildcat to become excited by these signs of some humbler creature of the woods.

But on reaching that scene of Skinny's memorable meeting with Hervey Willetts, Tom's keenest interest was aroused by something which he saw there, and which both of the others characteristically had failed to notice. Skinny, enthralled by his vision of the coveted badge, had been in no state for minute exploration, and as for Hervey, these things were quite out of his line. Besides, his sudden impulse of generosity toward Skinny would have been quite sufficient (as we know it was) to cause him to forget all else.

But Tom was as observant and methodical as Hervey was erratic, and as he paused to rest upon the log, he noticed how it lay directly across the path of the tracks. Thus the track line was broken for a couple of feet or so by this obstacle.

Supposing that the creature which had passed here had clambered over the log, Tom's scouting instinct was aroused to examine the rough bark carefully for any little tuft of hair which the animal might have left. And not finding any, he was puzzled. For by its tracks the creature must have been very small, certainly too small to have stepped, and not at all likely to have jumped over the log. If then it had clambered over the log it seemed remarkable that it had left no trace, not even a single hair, upon that rough surface.

Tom knew that this was unusual. He knew that old Uncle Jeb would laugh at him if he went back and said that some small creature had crawled over that nutmeg grater and left no sign of its crossing. He knew that no animal could graze a tree in its flight but old Uncle Jeb would find there some tell-tale souvenir of its passing.

Tom's interest was keenly aroused now. He was baffled and a little chagrined. But no supplementary inspection revealed so much as a single hair.

Thus confounded, he examined the tracks more carefully. He followed them up to where they emerged from the lower reaches of the mountain. Then he followed them back, aided where they were dim by the deeper prints of Hervey's shoes. Skinny sat upon the log waiting for him.

On the side of the log nearest the mountain the tracks turned and went sideways along the log for perhaps a yard to a point where the log was low and somewhat broken. Here, evidently, was where the animal had crossed. It must have been a very small animal, Tom thought, to have sought an easy place for crossing.

Having thus determined the exact place of crossing, Tom concentrated his attention on this spot, examining the bark systematically, inch by inch. But no vestige of a clew rewarded his microscopic scrutiny. He was baffled and his curiosity and determination rose in proportion to the difficulties. His big mouth was set tight, a menacing frown clouded his countenance, so that instinctively little Skinny refrained from speaking to him.

Tracing the apparent line of the animal's crossing over the log, Tom scrutinized the prints on the other side, that is, the side nearest camp. Here the prints were very clear by reason of the crust of mud caused by the dampness usually found near logs and fallen trees. Marks on this showed like marks on hard butter.

Suddenly Tom's attention was riveted by something directly under the apparent line of crossing, something which he had never seen the like of in all his woodland adventures since he had become a scout. What he saw looked singularly out of place there. Yet there it was printed in the hard crust of mud, and as clear as writing on a slate. No human footprint was near it. If a human being had made those marks that human being must have reached from the log to do it. And the printing was almost too nice for that.

Utterly dismayed, Tom looked again for human footprints but the nearest were those of Hervey on the other side of the log, some ten or a dozen feet beyond.

"Did either of you fellows do that?" Tom asked, pointing.

"Does—does it mean I can't have the badge?" Skinny asked, apprehensive of Tom's mood.

"Did either of you fellows do that?"

"N-no," Skinny answered timidly.

"Have you brought any one else up here?"

"Honest—I ain't."

"Well then," said Tom, with a kind of grim finality, "either some one else who didn't have any feet has been here or else that animal knows how to write. Look there."

Skinny obediently looked again. There below the log and close to the tracks were printed as clear as day the letters H. T. They were about two inches in size.

"Take your choice," said Tom with a kind of baffled conclusiveness which greatly impressed his little companion. *"Either those letters were printed there by some one who didn't have any feet, or else the animal knew how to write. Either one or the other. It's got me guessing."*

CHAPTER XXVII

THE GREATER MYSTERY

SINCE there was no solution of this singular puzzle, Tom did not let it continue to trouble him. He was too busy with his duties incidental to the closing season to concern himself with mysteries which were not likely to reveal anything of value. The kidnapping was a serious affair, and the curious discovery which he had made in the woods was soon relegated to the back of his mind by this, which was now the talk of the camp, and by his increasingly pressing labors.

Moreover he believed that some scout or other had visited this now memorable spot and marked his initials on the mud, squatting on the log the while. To be sure, the absence of footprints close by, save those easily recognizable as Skinny's, was

" DID EITHER OF YOU FELLOWS DO THAT ?" TOM ASKED.

Tom Slade on Mystery Trail. Page 151

perplexing, but since there was no other explanation, Tom accepted the one which seemed not wholly unlikely. At all events, what other explanation was there?

For an hour or more that same night Tom lay under Asbestos' elm pondering on his singular discovery. Then realizing that his duties were many and various, he put this matter out of his head altogether and went to work in the morning at the strenuous work of lowering and rolling up tents.

The papers which the boys brought up from Catskill that afternoon were full of the kidnapping. Master Harrington's distracted mother was under the care of a dozen or so specialists, six or eight servants had been discharged for neglect, Mr. Harrington offered a reward of five thousand dollars, somebody had seen the child in Detroit, another had seen him in Canada, another had seen him at a movie show, another had heard heart-rending cries in some marsh or other, and so on and so on.

In New York "an arrest was shortly expected," but it didn't arrive. The detectives were "saying nothing" and apparently doing nothing. Master

Anthony Harrington's picture was displayed on movie screens the country over.

But out of all this hodge-podge of cooked up news and irresponsible hints there remained just the one plausible clew to hang any hopes on and that was trainman Hanlon's recollection of seeing a child in a mackinaw jacket and carrying a jack-knife in the company of two men who alighted from a north-bound train at Catskill, within ten miles of Temple Camp.

One other item of news interested the camp community, and that was that boy scouts throughout the country had been asked to search for the missing child.

Meanwhile, the kidnappers sat tight, expecting no doubt that their demands for a large ransom would be more fruitful after the chances of legitimate rescue had been exhausted. The great fortune of Anthony Harrington of Wall Street was quite useless until a couple of ruffians chose to say the word. And meanwhile, Master Anthony, Jr., might be hacking himself all to pieces with a horrible jack-knife.

It was just when matters were at that stage that Pee-wee Harris, Elk Patrol, First Bridgeboro

Troop, went in swimming for the last time that summer in the cooling water of Black Lake. He gave a terrific cry, jumped on the springboard, howled for everybody to look, turned two complete somersaults and went kerplunk into the water with a mighty splash.

CHAPTER XXVIII

WATCHFUL WAITING

In a minute he came up sputtering and shouting. "What's that? A hunk of candy?" a scout sitting on the springboard called. For Pee-wee seldom returned from any adventure empty handed.

"A tu-shh-sphh——" Scout Harris answered.

"A which?"

"A turtshplsh—can't you hearshsph?"

"A what?"

"A turtlsh."

"A turtle?"

"Cantshunderstand Englsphish?"

He dragged himself up on the springboard dripping and spluttering, and clutching this latest memento of his submarine explorations.

"It's a turtle—t-u-r-t-e-l——I mean l-e—can't you understand English?" Pee-wee demanded as soon as the water was out of his mouth and nose.

"Not submarine English," his companion retorted. "You can't keep your mouth shut even under water."

It was indeed a turtle, which had already adopted tactics for a prolonged siege, its head, tail and four little stubby legs being drawn quite within its shell. Nor was it tempted out of this posture of defense when Pee-wee hurled it at Tom Slade who was standing near the mooring float, watching the diving.

"There's a souvenir for you, Tomasso," Pee-wee called.

Tom caught the turtle and was about to hurl it at another scout who stood a few yards distant, when he noticed something carved on the upper surface of the turtle's shell. He pulled up a tuft of grass, rubbing the shell to clean it, and as he did so, the carving came out clearly, showing the letters T. H.

The scout who had been ready to catch the missile now stepped over to look at it, and in ten seconds a dozen scouts were crowding around

Tom and craning their necks over his shoulders.

"Somebody's initials," Tom said without any suggestion of excitement.

"Maybe—maybe it was that kid who was kidnapped," Pee-wee vociferated.

"Only his initials are A. H.," Tom answered dully.

"No sooner said than stung," piped up one of the scouts.

"What'll we do with him? Keep him?" asked another.

"What good is he?" Tom said, apparently on the point of scaling the turtle into the lake. "Some scout or other cut his initials here, that's all. I don't see any use in keeping him; he isn't so very sociable."

"Lots of times you crawl in your shell and aren't so sociable, either," Pee-wee shot back at him. "I say let's keep him for a souvenir."

"We'll have a regular Bronx Park Zoo here pretty soon," a scout said. "We'll have to give him a name just like Asbestos."

Tom set the turtle on the ground and everybody waited silently. But the turtle was not to be beguiled out of his stronghold by any such strategy.

He remained as motionless as a stone. Pee-wee gave him a little poke with his foot but to no avail. They turned him around, setting him this way and that, they tried to pry his tail out but it went back like a spring.

They moved him a few yards distant in hopes that the change of scene might make him more sociable. But he showed no more sign of life than a fossil would have shown. So again they all waited. And they waited and waited and waited. They spoke in whispers and went on waiting.

But after a while this policy of watchful waiting became tiresome. Apparently the turtle was ready to withstand this siege for years if necessary. Disgustedly, one scout after another went away, and others came. Tempting morsels of food were placed in front of the turtle, in a bee line with his head.

"Gee whiz, if he doesn't care for food what *does* he care for?" Pee-wee observed, knowing the influence of food.

That settled it so far as he was concerned, and he went away, saying that the turtle was not human, or else that he was dead. Others, more patient, stood about, waiting. And all the famed ingenuity of scouts was exhausted to beguile or to drive the turtle out of his stronghold. At one time as many as twenty scouts surrounded him, with sticks, with food, and Scouty, the camp dog, came down and danced around and made a great fuss and went away thoroughly disgusted.

The turtle was master of the situation.

CHAPTER XXIX

THE WANDERING MINSTREL

With one exception the most patient scout at Temple Camp was Westy Martin of the interesting Bridgeboro, New Jersey, Troop. He could sit huddled up in a bush for an hour studying a bird. He could sit and fish for hours without catching anything. But the turtle was too much for him.

"We ought to name that guy Llewellyn," he commented, as he strolled away; "that means *lightning,* according to some book or other. There was an old Marathon racer a couple of million years ago named Llewellyn."

"That's a good name for him," Tom admitted.

"You going to hang around, Slady?"

"I'm going to fight it out on these lines if it takes all summer," Tom said.

Thus the two most patient, stubborn living things in all the world were left alone together— the turtle and Tom Slade.

Tom sat on a rock and the turtle sat on the ground. Tom did not budge. Neither did the turtle. The turtle was facing up toward the camp and away from the lake. Tom rested his chin in his hands, studying the initials on the turtle's shell. If they had been A. H. instead of T. H. they would indeed have been the very initials of Master Anthony Harrington, Jr. But a miss is as good as a mile, thought Tom, and T. H. is no more like A. H. than it is like Z. Q.

This train of thought naturally recalled to his mind the letters he had seen imprinted in the mud up in the woods. But those letters were H. T. and there was therefore no connection between these three sets of letters.

Tom knew well enough the habit of the Temple Camp scouts of carving their initials everywhere. The rough bench where they waited for the mail wagon to come along was covered with initials. And among them Tom recalled a certain sprightly tenderfoot, Theodore Howell by name, who had been at camp early that same season. Doubtless this artistic triumph on the bulging back of Llewellyn was the handiwork of that same tenderfoot.

And likely enough, too, those letters up in the woods were the initials of Harry Thorne, still at camp. Tom would ask Harry about that. And at the same time he would remind some of these carvers in wood and clay not to leave any artistic memorials on the camp woodwork. It was part of Tom's work to look after matters of that kind. About the only conclusion he reached from these two disconnected sets of initials was that he would have an eye out for specialists in carving. . . .

But Tom's authority was as naught when it came to Llewellyn. The turtle cared not for the young camp assistant. He sat upon the ground motionless as a rock, apparently dead to the world.

Tom had now no more interest in the turtle than a kind of sporting instinct not to be beaten. He could sit upon the rock as long as his adversary could sit upon the ground. In a moment of exasperation he had been upon the point of hurling the turtle into the lake, but had refrained, and now he was reconciled to a vigil which should last all night.

Llewellyn had met his match.

For fifty-seven minutes by his watch, Tom waited. Then the tip end of Llewellyn's nose emerged slowly, cautiously, and remained stationary.

Eleven minutes of tense silence elapsed.

Then the tip end of Llewellyn's nose emerged a trifle more, stopped, started again and lo, his whole head and neck were out, craned stiffly upward toward the camp.

Tom did not move a muscle, he hardly breathed. Soon the turtle's tail was sticking straight out and one forward claw was emerging slowly, doubtfully.

Silence.

Another claw emerged and the neck relaxed its posture of listening reconnoissance. Then, presto, Llewellyn was waddling around like a lumbering old ferry boat and heading straight for the lake. As he waddled along in a bee line something which Tom had once read came flashing into his mind, which was that no matter where a turtle is placed, be it in the middle of the Desert of Sahara, he will travel a bee line for the nearest water.

But his recollection of this was as nothing to Tom now, when he saw with mingled feelings of shame and excitement something which seemed to open a way to the most dramatic possibilities.

As the turtle entered the muddy area near the lake Tom realized, what he should have known before, that the tracks which Hervey Willetts had followed from the mountain and which Skinny had followed from the lake were the tracks of a turtle! *The tracks of a turtle coming from a locality where it did not belong, straight for the still water which was its natural element.*

With a quick inspiration Tom darted forward into the mud catching the turtle just as it was waddling into the water. He did not know why he did this, it was just upon an impulse, and in making the sudden reach he all but lost his balance. As it was he had to swing both arms to keep his feet, and as he did so the turtle fell upside down in the drier mud a few feet back from shore. As Tom lifted it, there, imprinted in the mud were the letters H. T.

The initials T. H. on the creature's back had been reversed when he fell upside down. And Tom realized with a thrill that what had just happened before his eyes had happened at that log up in the woods.

Llewellyn, the Humpty-dumpty of the animal world, had slid off the log, alighting upside down.

For a moment Tom Slade paused in dismay.

So Teddy Howell and Harry Thorne had nothing to do with this. This lumbering, waddling creature had come flopping along down out of the silent lower reaches of that frowning mountain, straight to his destination. He was not the first printer to print something the wrong way around.

Who, then, was T. H.? Not Master Anthony, Jr., at all events. But some one afar off, surely. Abstractedly, Tom Slade gazed off toward that towering mountain whence this clumsy but unerring messenger had come. It looked very dark up there. Tom recalled how from those lofty crags the great eagle had swooped down and met his match before the hallowed little home of Orestes.

In a kind of reverie Tom's thoughts wandered to Orestes. Orestes would be in bed by now. Orestes had lived away up near where that turtle had come from. And the thought of Llewellyn and Orestes turned Tom's thought to Hervey Willetts.   He had not seen much of Hervey the last day or two. . . .

Tom fixed his gaze upon that old monarch where again the first crimson rays of dying sunlight glinted the pinnacles of the somber pines near its summit.   How solemn, how still, it seemed up there.   The nearer sounds about the camp seemed only to emphasize that brooding silence.   It was like the silence of some vast cathedral—awful in its majestic solitude.

And this impassive, stolid, hard-shell pilgrim, knowing his business like the bully scout he was, had come stumbling, sliding, rolling and waddling down out of those fastnesses, because there was something right here which he wanted.   And he had brought a clew.   Should the human scout be found wanting where this humble little hero had triumphed?

"I never paid much attention to those stories," Tom mused; "but if there's a draft dodger living up there, I'm going to find him.   If there's a hermit I'm going to see him.   If there's . . ."

He paused suddenly in his musing, listening. It was the distant voice of a scout returning to camp.   He was singing one of those crazy songs that he was famous for. Tom looked up beyond the supply cabin and saw him coming down, twirling his hat on a stick, hitching up one stocking as often as it went down—carefree, happy-go-lucky, delightfully heedless.

He looked for all the world like a ragged vagabond. The evening breeze bore the strain he was singing down to where stolid Tom stood and he smiled, then suddenly became tensely interested as he listened. Tom often wondered where Hervey got his songs and ballads. On the present occasion this is what the blithe minstrel was caroling:

> Saint Anthony he was a saint,
>   And he was thin and bony;
> His mother called him Anthonee,
>   But the kids they called him Tony.

CHAPTER XXX

HERVEY MAKES A PROMISE

"Tony!"
The word reached Tom's ears like a pistol shot.
Tony.

> His mother called him Anthonee,
> And the kids they called him Tony.

Anthony—Tony. Why, of course, Tony was the universal nickname for Anthony. And if any kids were allowed within the massive iron gates at the Harrington Estate, undoubtedly they called him Tony.

Tom, holding the turtle like a big rubber stamp, printed the letters several times on the ground—H. T. He scrutinized them, in their proper order on the turtle's back—T. H. Tony Harrington.

Could it be? Could it really mean anything in connection with that lost child? Was it possible that while Detective Something-or-other, and Lieutenant Thing-um-bob, and Sheriff Bullhead and Captain Fuss-and-feathers were all giving interviews to newspaper men, this sturdy little messenger was coming down to camp with a clew, straight from the hiding place of a pair of ruffians and a little boy with a——

With a new jack-knife!

Tom was thrilled by this fresh thought. For half a minute he stood just where he was, hardly knowing what to do, what to think.

"You're a good scout, Llewellyn," he finally mused aloud; "old Rough and Ready—slow but sure. Do you know what you did, you clumsy old ice wagon? You brought a second-class scout badge and an Eagle award with you. And I'd like to know if you brought anything else of value. That's what I would."

But Llewellyn did not hear, at least he did not seem at all impressed. His head, claws and tail were drawn in again. He had changed himself into a rock. He was a good detective, because he knew how to keep still.

Tom strolled up to supper, as excited as it was in his nature to be, and greatly preoccupied.

On his way up he dropped Llewellyn into Tenderfoot Pond, a diminutive sheet of water, so named in honor of the diminutive scout contingent at camp. He would have room enough to spend the balance of his life resting after his arduous and memorable journey. And there he still abides, by last accounts, monarch of the mud and water, and suns himself for hours at a time on a favorite rock. He is ranked as a scout of the first-class, as indeed he should be, but he is frightfully lazy. He is a one stunt scout, as they say, but immensely popular. One hundred dollars in cash was offered for him and refused, so you can tell by that.

After supper Tom sought out Hervey. "Herve," he said, "I don't suppose you ever tried your hand at keeping a secret, did you? Where's your Eagle badge?"

"My patrol has got it."

"Well, if you can't keep a badge do you think you can keep a secret? You were telling me you wouldn't let a girl wear an honor badge of yours——"

"That was three days ago I told you that. Girls are different from what they were then. Can you balance a scout staff on your nose?"

"I never tried that. Listen, Hervey, and promise you won't tell anybody. I'm telling you because I know I can trust you and because I like you and I think you can help me. I want you to do something for me, will you?"

"Suppose while I'm doing it I should decide I'd rather do something else? You know how I am."

"Well, in that case," said Tom soberly, "you get a large rock tied to your neck by a double sailor's knot, and are gently lowered into Black Lake."

"I can undo a double sailor's knot under water," said Hervey.

Tom laughed in spite of himself. "Hervey," said he, "do you know what kind of tracks those were you followed?"

" A killyloo bird's?"

"They were the tracks of a turtle and I was a fool not to know it. That turtle had the letters T. H. carved on his shell. Do you know what those letters might possibly stand for?"

"Terrible Hustler? How many guesses do I have?"

"Those letters were printed wrong way around in the mud up near that log when the turtle fell off the log upside down," Tom continued soberly.

"He fell all over himself, hey?"

"You didn't happen to notice those letters up there, did you?"

"Not guilty."

"It's best always to keep your eyes open," Tom said.

"Not always, Slady."

"Yes, always."

"When you're asleep?"

Tom was a trifle nettled. "Well, are you willing to help me or not?" he asked.

"Slady, I'm yours sincerely forever."

"Well then, meet me under Asbestos' elm tree at quarter of eleven, and keep your mouth shut about it. We're going to see if we can find Anthony Harrington, Jr."

"T. H.?"

"Tony is nickname for Anthony; you just said so in your song."

"When my soul burst forth in gladness, hey?

The scout Caruso, hey, Slady? What are we going to meet under the elm tree for?"

"You'll see when we get there. All you have to do in the meantime is to keep still. Do you think you can do that?"

"Silence is my middle name, Slady; I eat it alive."

CHAPTER XXXI

SHERLOCK NOBODY HOLMES

SINCE Tom Slade, camp assistant, said it would be all right for Hervey to meet him at quarter of eleven under the elm tree, Hervey was only too glad to jump the rule, which was that scouts must turn in at ten thirty, directly after camp-fire. This stealthy meeting under the old elm tree near the witching hour of midnight was quite to Hervey's taste.

He found Tom already there.

"Now for the buried treasure, hey, Slady?" he said.

"I want you to promise me not to sing," Tom said soberly. "Now listen," he added, whispering. "That turtle came from way up in that mountain. It has T. H. cut on its shell, and I think the carving is new. That trainman said two men with a kid got out at Catskill. He said the kid had a jack-knife. His folks said he had a sweater. Maybe the men put the jacket on him —keep still till I get through. Maybe they wanted to disguise him.

"It's bad enough for detectives to make fools of themselves and get that kid's family all excited, without scouts doing it. Maybe I'm all wrong but we're going to make sure."

"Are you going up there, Slady?" Hervey whispered excitedly, as if ready to start.

"No, not yet. We're going to find out something about the sweater first."

"No one is in this but just you and I, hey?"

"And Llewellyn and Orestes. Now listen, I want you to climb up this tree and don't scare the bird whatever you do. You can climb like a monkey. Don't interfere with the nest, but feel with your fingers and see if you can give me an idea what that red streak is made of. Don't call down. All we know now is that Orestes and Llewellyn came from pretty near the same spot. Two little clews are better than one big one if they match. Go on now, beat it, and whatever you do don't call down or I'll murder you."

Hardly a rustling of the branches Tom heard as the young scout ascended. One silent leaf fluttered down and blew in his face. That was all. A minute, perhaps two minutes, elapsed. Then Tom saw the agile form slowly descending the dark trunk.

"I'd make a good sneak thief, hey?" Hervey whispered.

"You're a wonder on climbing," Tom said, with frank admiration.

"It's kind of like worsted, Slady," Hervey whispered, as he brushed the bark from his clothing. "It's all woven in with other stuff but it feels like —sort of like worsted. I put my flashlight on it, it's faded—"

"I know it is," Tom said, "but it was bright red when we first saw it and that's what makes me think it hasn't been in the nest long. I don't believe it had been there more than a couple of days or so when we found the nest. All I want to know now is whether it's wool, or anything like that. You think it is?"

"Sure it is."

"All right, then one thing more and we'll hit the trail. You meet me in the morning right after breakfast."

CHAPTER XXXII

THE BEGINNING OF THE JOURNEY

EARLY the next morning Tom and Hervey hiked down to Catskill.

"I don't see why we don't hike straight for the mountain," Hervey said; "it would be much nearer."

"Didn't you ever sail up the Hudson?" Tom asked him. "All the trails up the steep mountains are as plain as day from the river. If you want to discover a trail get a bird's-eye view. Don't you know that aviators discover trails that even hunters never knew about before? If the kidnappers went up that mountain, they probably went an easy way, because they're not scouts or woodsmen. See? It would be an awful job picking our way up that mountain from camp.

If those men are up that way they knew where they were going. They're not pioneers, they're kidnappers."

"Slady, you're a wonder."

"Except when it comes to climbing trees," Tom said.

At Catskill they hired a skiff and rowed out to about the middle of the river. From there Hervey was greatly surprised at what he saw. His bantering mood was quieted at last and he became sober as Tom, holding the oar handles with one hand, pointed up to a mountain behind the bordering heights along the river. Upon this, as upon others, were the faintest suggestions of lines. No trails were to be seen, of course; only wriggling lines of shadow, as they seemed, now visible, now half visible, now fading out altogether like breath on a piece of glass.

It seemed incredible that mere paths, often all but undiscernible close at hand, should be distinguishable from this distance. But there they were, and it needed only visual concentration upon them to perceive that they were not well defined paths to be sure, but thin, faint lines of shadow. They lacked substance, but there they were.

"That's old Tyrant," Tom said. "See?"

Hervey would never have recognized the mountain. The side of it which they saw was not at all like the familiar side which faced Temple Camp. That frowning, jungle-covered ascent seemed less forbidding from the river, but how Tom could identify it was beyond Hervey's comprehension.

It was apparent that by following a road which began at Catskill they would skirt the mountain along its less precipitous ascent, and Tom assumed that the trail, so doubtfully and elusively marked upon the height, would be easily discoverable where it left the road, as undoubtedly it did.

Deduction and calculation were not at all in Hervey's line; he would have been quite satisfied to plunge into the interminable thicket on the side near camp and get lost there.

"You see there is more than one way to kill a cat," Tom observed. "I was thinking of the kidnappers while you were thinking about the mountain. As long as they went up I thought I might as well let them show us the easy way."

"You're a wonder, Slady!"

"There are two sides to every mountain," Tom said.

"Like every story, hey?"

"You're a good scout only you don't use your brain enough. You use your hands and feet and your heart, I can't deny that."

"The pleasure is mine," said Hervey. "We're going to sneak up the back way, hey?"

"No, we're going up the front way," Tom smiled. "Llewellyn came down the back way."

"He's a peach of a scout, hey?"

"The best ever."

Hervey had soon a pretty good demonstration of the advantage of using the brain first and the hands and feet afterwards. And he had a pretty good demonstration of the particular kind of scout that Tom Slade was—a scout that thinks.

They hit into the road about fifty yards from the boat landing and followed it through a valley to where it ran along the foot of the mountain.

"Are you sure this is the right mountain?" Hervey asked. "They all look alike when you get close to them."

"Yop," said Tom; "what do you think of it?"

"Oh, I'm not particular about mountains," Hervey said.   "They all look alike to me."

Following the road, they watched the bordering woods on the mountainside carefully for any sign of a trail.   Several times they clambered up into the thicket supposing some tiny clearing or sparse area to be the beginning of the winding way they sought.

Hervey was thoroughly aroused now and serious.   Once they picked their way up into the woods for perhaps a dozen yards, only to find themselves in a jungle with no sign of trail.   Tom returned down out of these blind alleys, his hands scratched, his clothing torn, and resumed his way along the road doggedly, saying little.   He knew it was somewhere and he was going to find it.

Suddenly he paused by a certain willow tree, looking at it curiously.

"What is it?" Hervey asked excitedly.

"Looks as if a jack-knife had been at work around here, huh?   Somebody's been making a willow whistle.   Look at this."

Tom held up a little tube of moist willow bark, at the same time kicking some shavings at his

feet. "Looks as if they passed this point, anyway," he said. "Ever make one of those willow
whistles? I've made dozens of them for tenderfeet. If you make them the right way, they make
a dickens of a loud noise."

CHAPTER XXXIII

THE CLIMB

AT last they found the trail. It wound up and away from the road about half a mile farther along than where they had found the shavings.

"I guess no one would have noticed those but you," Hervey said admiringly; "I guess the detectives would have gone right past them."

"A lot of little clews are better than one big one," Tom said as they scrambled up into the dense thicket. "The initials on the turtle, the new jack-knife, the willow shavings, all fit together."

"Yes, but it takes Tom Slade to fit them together," Hervey said.

"Maybe we might be mistaken after all," Tom answered. "Anyway, nobody'll have the laugh on us. We didn't talk to reporters."

Their journey now led up through dense woods, but the trail was clear and easy to follow. Now and again they caught glimpses of the country below and could see the majestic Hudson winding like a broad silver ribbon away between other mountains.

"Hark!" Tom said, stopping short.

Hervey paused, spellbound.

"I guess it was only a boat whistling," Tom said.

"It's pretty lonesome up here," Hervey commented.

The side of the mountain which they were ascending was less precipitous than the side facing the camp, and save for occasional patches of thicket where the path was overgrown, their way was not difficult.

"But I think it's longer than the trip would be straight from camp," Hervey said.

"Sure it is," Tom said; "Llewellyn proves that; he went down the shortest way. He might have come down this way to the Hudson, only he hit a bee line for the nearest water."

After about three quarters of an hour of this wearisome climb they came out on the edge of a lofty minor cliff which commanded a panoramic view of Temple Camp. They were, in fact, close to the edge of the more precipitous ascent and near the very point whence the eagle had swooped down.

From this spot the path descended into the thicket and down the steep declivity. Below them lay Black Lake with tiny black specks upon it—canoes manned by scouts. The faintest suggestion of human voices could be heard, but they did not sound human; rather like voices from another world.

Suddenly, in the vast, solemn stillness below them a shrill whistling sounded clear out of the dense jungle. It might have been a hundred yards down, or fifty; Tom could not say.

He was not at all excited nor elated. Holding up one hand to warn Hervey to silence, he stood waiting, listening intently.

Again the whistle sounded, shrill, clear-cut, in the still morning air.

CHAPTER XXXIV

THE RESCUE

"TAKE off your shoes and leave them here," Tom whispered; "and follow me and don't speak. Step just where I step."

Tom's soft moccasins were better even than stocking feet and he moved down into the thicket stealthily, silently. Not a twig cracked beneath his feet. He lifted the impediments of branch and bush aside and let them spring easily back into place again without a sound. Hervey crawled close behind him, passing through these openings while Tom held the entangled thicket apart for both to pass. He moved like a panther. Never in all his life had Hervey Willetts seen such an exhibition of scouting.

Presently Tom paused, holding open the brush.

"Hervey," he said in the faintest whisper, "they say you're happy-go-lucky. Are you willing to risk your life—again?"

"I'm yours sincerely forever, Slady."

"We're going home the short way; we're going down the way the turtle did," Tom whispered. "It's the only way—look. Shh."

With heart thumping in his breast, Hervey looked down where Tom pointed and saw amid the dense thicket a glint of bright red. Even as he looked, it moved, and appeared again in another tiny opening of the thicket close by.

"What is it?" he whispered.

"A. H." Tom hardly breathed. "It's little Anthony Harrington—shh. Don't speak from now on; just follow me. See this trickle of water? There's a spring down there. They can't have their camp there, they'd roll down. The kid is there alone. If you're not willing to tackle the descent, say so. If we go down the regular way we'll have them after us. We've got to go a way that they *can't* go. Say the word. Are you game?"

"You heard them call me a dare-devil, didn't you?" Hervey whispered. "They claim I don't care anything about the Eagle award. They're right. I'd rather be a dare-devil. Go ahead and don't ask foolish questions."

For about twenty yards Tom descended, stealthily pausing every few feet or so. Hervey was behind him and could not see what Tom saw. He did not venture to speak.

Then Tom paused, holding the brush open, and peering through—thoughtfully, intently. He looked like a scout in a picture. Hervey waited behind him, his heart in his throat. He could not have stood there if Tom had not been in front of him. It seemed interminable, this waiting. But Tom was not the one to leap without looking.

Suddenly, like a flash of lightning, he threw aside all stealth and caution and, tearing the bushes out of his path, darted forward like a hunted animal. Hervey could only follow, his heart beating, his nerves tingling with excitement. What happened, seemed all in an instant. It was over almost before it began. Tom had emerged into a little clearing where there was a spring and the next thing Hervey knew, there was his companion stuffing a handkerchief into the mouth of a little fellow in a red sweater and lifting the little form into his arms.

Hervey saw the clearing, the spring, the handkerchief stuffed into the child's mouth, the little legs dangling as Tom carried the struggling form —he saw these things as in a kind of vision.   The next thing he noticed (and that was when they had descended forty or fifty yards below the spring) was that the child's sweater was frayed near the shoulder.

Down the steep declivity Tom moved, over rocks, now crawling, now letting himself down, now handing himself by one hand from tree to tree, agilely, carefully, surely.   Now he relieved one arm by taking the child in the other, always using his free hand to let himself down through that precipitous jungle.   Never once did he speak or pause until he had left an almost perpendicular area of half a mile or so of rock and jungle between them and the spring above.

Then, breathless, he paused in a little level space above a great rock and set the child down.

"Don't be frightened, Tony," he said; "we're going to take you home.   And don't scream when

I take this handkerchief out because that will spoil it all."

"Is it safe to stop here?" Hervey asked.

"Sure, they'll go down the path when they want to hunt for him. They'll never get down here. The mountain is with us now."

"I didn't drop my whistle," the little fellow piped up, as if that were his chief concern.

"Good," said Tom, in an effort to interest him and put him at ease. "That's a dandy whistle; tell us about it. Because we're your friends, you know."

"Am I going to see my mother and father?"

"You bet. Away down there is a big camp where there are lots of boys and you're going to stay there till they come and get you."

"They sent me to the spring to get water and I took my whistle so I could soak it in the water, because that makes it go good. I made it myself, that whistle."

Tom, his clothes torn, his face and hands bleeding from scratches, sat upon the edge of a big rock with the little fellow drawn tight against him.

"And when you whistled we came and got you, hey? That's the kind of fellows we are. And

I bet I know how that nice sweater got frayed, too. A little bird did that."

"I left it hanging on a tree near the spring when they sent me to get water," the boy said, "and I left it there all night." He poked his finger in the frayed place as if he were proud of it.

"And I'll show you who did it," Tom said; "because that little thief is right down there in that big camp. And I'll show you the turtle you carved your initials on too. Because he came to our camp, too. There's so much fun there. And you're going to step very carefully and hold on to me, and we're going down, down, down, till we get to that camp where there is a man that knows how to make dandy crullers. I bet you like crullers?"

A camp where even birds and turtles go, and where they know how to make crullers, was a magic place, not to be missed by any means. And little Anthony Harrington was already undecided as to whether he would rather live there than at home.

CHAPTER THE LAST

Y-EXTRA! Y-EXTRA!

THE ragged little newsboys in the big city shouted themselves hoarse. "Y-extree! Y-extra! Anthony Harrington safe! Rescued by Boy Scouts! Y-extree! Mister!"

And those who bought the extras learned how the kidnappers of Anthony Harrington allowed him to purchase for nine cents a turtle from a little farm boy whom he met at the station at Catskill. And of how that turtle walked off and gave the whole thing away. Llewellyn and Orestes got even more credit than Tom Slade, but he did not care, for a scout is a brother to every other scout, and it was all in the family.

And so, as I said in the beginning, if you should visit Temple Camp, you will hear the story told of how Llewellyn, scout of the first-class, and Orestes, winner of the merit badges for architecture and music, were by their scouting skill and lore instrumental in solving a mystery and performing a great good turn.

They are still there, the two of them; one in her elm, the other in Tenderfoot Pond. And Orestes (but this is strictly confidential) has a little scout troop of her own, tenderfeet with a vengeance, for they are out of the eggs scarcely ten days.

THE END

THE TOM SLADE BOOKS

By PERCY KEESE FITZHUGH

Author of "Roy Blakeley," "Pee-wee Harris," "Westy Martin," Etc.

Illustrated. Individual Picture Wrappers in Colors. Every Volume Complete in Itself.

"Let your boy grow up with Tom Slade," is a suggestion which thousands of parents have followed during the past, with the result that the TOM SLADE BOOKS are the most popular boys' books published today. They take Tom Slade through a series of typical boy adventures through his tenderfoot days as a scout, through his gallant days as an American doughboy in France, back to his old patrol and the old camp ground at Black Lake, and so on.

TOM SLADE, BOY SCOUT
TOM SLADE AT TEMPLE CAMP
TOM SLADE ON THE RIVER
TOM SLADE WITH THE COLORS
TOM SLADE ON A TRANSPORT
TOM SLADE WITH THE BOYS OVER
                            THERE
TOM SLADE, MOTORCYCLE DISPATCH
                            BEARER
TOM SLADE WITH THE FLYING CORPS
TOM SLADE AT BLACK LAKE
TOM SLADE ON MYSTERY TRAIL
TOM SLADE'S DOUBLE DARE
TOM SLADE ON OVERLOOK MOUNTAIN
TOM SLADE PICKS A WINNER
TOM SLADE AT BEAR MOUNTAIN

GROSSET & DUNLAP,   PUBLISHERS,   NEW YORK

THE ROY BLAKELEY BOOKS

By PERCY KEESE FITZHUGH

Author of "Tom Slade," "Pee-wee Harris," "Westy Martin," Etc.

Illustrated. Individual Picture Wrappers in Color.
Every Volume Complete in Itself.

In the character and adventures of Roy Blakeley are typified the very essence of Boy life. He is a real boy, as real as Huck Finn and Tom Sawyer. He is the moving spirit of the troop of Scouts of which he is a member, and the average boy has to go only a little way in the first book before Roy is the best friend he ever had, and he is willing to part with his best treasure to get the next book in the series.

ROY·BLAKELEY

ROY BLAKELEY'S ADVENTURES IN CAMP

ROY BLAKELEY, PATHFINDER

ROY BLAKELEY'S CAMP ON WHEELS

ROY BLAKELEY'S SILVER FOX PATROL

ROY BLAKELEY'S MOTOR CARAVAN

ROY BLAKELEY, LOST, STRAYED OR STOLEN

ROY BLAKELEY'S BEE-LINE HIKE

ROY BLAKELEY AT THE HAUNTED CAMP

ROY BLAKELEY'S FUNNY BONE HIKE

ROY BLAKELEY'S TANGLED TRAIL

ROY BLAKELEY ON THE MOHAWK TRAIL

GROSSET & DUNLAP, PUBLISHERS, NEW YORK

THE PEE-WEE HARRIS BOOKS
By PERCY KEESE FITZHUGH
Author of "Tom Slade," "Roy Blakeley," "Westy Martin," Etc.

**Illustrated. Individual Picture Wrappers in Color.
Every Volume Complete in Itself.**

All readers of the Tom Slade and the Roy Blakeley books are acquainted with Pee-wee Harris. These stories record the true facts concerning his size (what there is of it) and his heroism (such as it is), his voice, his clothes, his appetite, his friends, his enemies, his victims. Together with the thrilling narrative of how he foiled, baffled, circumvented and triumphed over everything and everybody (except where he failed) and how even when he failed he succeeded. The whole recorded in a series of screams and told with neither muffler nor cut-out.

PEE-WEE HARRIS

PEE-WEE HARRIS ON THE TRAIL

PEE-WEE HARRIS IN CAMP

PEE-WEE HARRIS IN LUCK

PEE-WEE HARRIS ADRIFT

PEE-WEE HARRIS F. O. B. BRIDGEBORO

PEE-WEE HARRIS FIXER

PEE-WEE HARRIS: AS GOOD AS HIS WORD

GROSSET & DUNLAP,   PUBLISHERS,   NEW YORK

EVERY BOY'S LIBRARY
BOY SCOUT EDITION

The books in this library have been proven by nation-wide canvass to be the one most universally in demand by the boys themselves. Originally published in more expensive editions only, they are now re-issued at a lower price so that all boys may have the advantage of reading and owning them. It is the only series of books published under the control of this great organization, whose sole object is the welfare and happiness of the boy himself.

Adventures in Beaver Stream Camp, Major A. R. Dugmore

Along the Mohawk Trail, Percy Keese Fitzhugh

Animal Heroes, Ernest Thompson Seton

Baby Elton, Quarter-Back, Leslie W. Quirk

Bartley, Freshman Pitcher, William Heyliger

Billy Topsail with Doctor Luke of the Labrador, Norman Duncan

The Biography of a Grizzly, Ernest Thompson Seton

The Boy Scouts of Black Eagle Patrol, Leslie W. Quirk

The Boy Scouts of Bob's Hill, Charles Pierce Burton

Brown Wolf and Other Stories, Jack London

Buccaneers and Pirates of Our Coasts, Frank R. Stockton

The Call of the Wild, Jack London

Cattle Ranch to College, R. Doubleday

College Years, Ralph D. Paine

Cruise of the Cachalot, Frank T. Bullen

The Cruise of the Dazzler, Jack London

Don Strong, Patrol Leader, W. Heyliger

Don Strong of the Wolf Patrol, William Heyliger

For the Honor of the School, Ralph Henry Barbour

The Gaunt Gray Wolf, Dillon Wallace

Grit-a-Plenty, Dillon Wallace

The Guns of Europe, Joseph A. Altsheler

The Half-Back, Ralph Henry Barbour

Handbook for Boys, Revised Edition Boy Scouts of America

The Horsemen of the Plains, Joseph A. Altsheler

Jim Davis, John Masefield

Kidnapped, Robert Louis Stevenson

Last of the Chiefs, Joseph A. Altsheler

The Last of the Mohicans, James Fenimore Cooper

Last of the Plainsmen, Zane Grey

Lone Bull's Mistake, J. W. Shultz

Pete, The Cow Puncher, J. B. Ames

The Quest of the Fish-Dog Skin, James W. Schultz

Ranche on the Oxhide, Henry Inman

The Ransom of Red Chief and Other O. Henry Stories for Boys, Edited by F. K. Mathiews

Scouting With Daniel Boone, Everett T. Tomlinson

Scouting With Kit Carson, Everett T. Tomlinson

Through College on Nothing a Year, Christian Gauss

Treasure Island, Robert Louis Stevenson

20,000 Leagues Under the Sea, Jules Verne

Under Boy Scout Colors, J. B. Ames

Ungava Bob, Dillon Wallace

GROSSET & DUNLAP, Publishers, NEW YORK